SPY PUPS
DANGER ISLAND

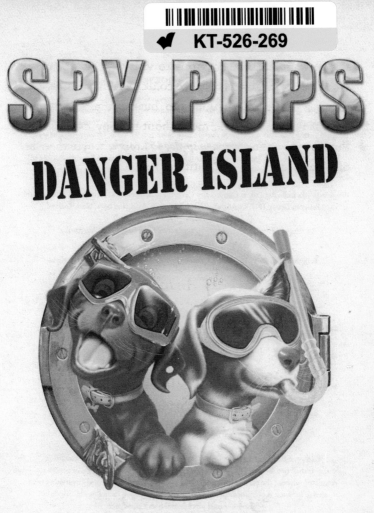

ANDREW COPE

Illustrated by James de la Rue

PUFFIN

PUFFIN BOOKS

Published by the Penguin Group
Penguin Books Ltd, 80 Strand, London WC2R ORL, England
Penguin Group (USA) Inc., 375 Hudson Street, New York, New York 10014, USA
Penguin Group (Canada), 90 Eglinton Avenue East, Suite 700, Toronto, Ontario, Canada M4P 2Y3
(a division of Pearson Penguin Canada Inc.)
Penguin Ireland, 25 St Stephen's Green, Dublin 2, Ireland (a division of Penguin Books Ltd)
Penguin Group (Australia), 250 Camberwell Road, Camberwell, Victoria 3124, Australia
(a division of Pearson Australia Group Pty Ltd)
Penguin Books India Pvt Ltd, 11 Community Centre, Panchsheel Park, New Delhi – 110 017, India
Penguin Group (NZ), 67 Apollo Drive, Rosedale, Auckland 0632, New Zealand
(a division of Pearson New Zealand Ltd)
Penguin Books (South Africa) (Pty) Ltd, 24 Sturdee Avenue, Rosebank,
Johannesburg 2196, South Africa

Penguin Books Ltd, Registered Offices: 80 Strand, London WC2R ORL, England

puffinbooks.com

First published 2011

004

Text copyright © Andrew Cope, 2011
Illustrations copyright © James de la Rue, 2011
All rights reserved

The moral right of the author and illustrator has been asserted

Set in Bembo Book MT Std 15/18 pt
Typeset by Palimpsest Book Production Limited, Falkirk, Stirlingshire
Made and printed in Great Britain by Clays Ltd, St Ives plc

British Library Cataloguing in Publication Data
A CIP catalogue record for this book is available from the British Library

ISBN: 978-0-141-32606-1

www.greenpenguin.co.uk

ALWAYS LEARNING   **PEARSON**

To all those who think they can't.
Guess what?
You're wrong!

Global thanks and hellos

For Meg, Gareth and Emma . . . I hope this
book reaches you in South Africa?

For Kaavya. Thanks for looking after me in
Delhi

And for Em and Harry Duffy. New Zealand?
Great move!

Message to all of you . . . keep reading, it's
great for your brain.

x

Contents

1. Monster from the Deep

'There you go, boy,' said the man, kneeling down to unclip the dog's lead. 'Go and have a scamper on the beach.'

The small dog darted off, leaving doggy paw prints in the sand. The dog didn't mind that it was nearly midnight. Nor did the man. The seaside made him feel like a teenager and he was so excited he couldn't sleep. It was a beautiful August night. Short-sleeves weather. The full moon shimmered across the ocean, which roared in the background. The man removed his shoes and socks and squeezed the cool sand between his toes. He strolled to the water's edge where the waves pounded the shore, then skipped backwards like a child to avoid the froth. The man couldn't help but grin. He loved holidays.

His dog ran across the sand, chasing a crab. The man picked up a stick and called to his pet. He threw the stick towards the sea and the dog tore after it, returning quickly, ready for more. 'OK, boy,' said the man, bending to pick up the stick. 'One more throw and then we really must get some shut-eye.' He hurled the stick towards the water. 'Go, Timmy,' he encouraged. 'Fetch!'

The dog started after the stick. Then it stopped suddenly. 'Go on, boy,' laughed the man. 'You love swimming, remember?' The moon disappeared behind a cloud, casting the beach into darkness. Timmy growled. Without the moonlight the man couldn't see his dog. Instead he heard a snarl and a yelp of fear. 'What's up, Timmy?' he shouted. 'Where are you, boy?'

With no silvery moonlight the sea was now a seething black mass, with white waves crashing to shore. The man wasn't sure whether it was due to the cold or fear, but he pulled up his collar. As he stepped towards the sea, Timmy shot past him, howling in terror, his tail between his legs.

The man felt a chill run down his spine. 'What on earth . . .?' he began, peering at the ocean. He froze with fear. A huge black creature reared up and glared at him. It groaned and revealed razor-sharp teeth. As the monster lunged towards him the man put his hands to his face to protect himself. He'd never seen such a terrifying sight. But instead of attacking him the creature dived back into the ocean, creating a huge wave that knocked the man off his feet. The cold water brought him to his senses and he jumped up and ran, yelping louder than his dog.

2. August is Gloop

'I've got bigger fish to fry, sir,' explained the police officer. 'Every news reporter and camera crew in the country is in town. They're saying it's another hit by the "Toxic Terror". All I know is that if I ever get my hands on whoever it is, they'll know what terror is!'

'So you're not going to investigate the monster?' asked the man. 'It was huge, I'm telling you. Black, with massive teeth.' The man opened his mouth and pointed, in case the policeman didn't understand what teeth were. 'It even terrified my dog! I thought I was a goner.'

The policeman shook his head. 'I've taken your statement, sir, and we'll look into it as soon as the dust has settled on this little crisis.' He waved his arm around the beach.

'But don't you see?' said the man. 'There's a monster lurking out there, officer. A killer. It's not safe to swim! You must warn the tourists!'

The policeman sighed and snapped his notebook shut. 'Sir,' he began, 'your monster from the black lagoon was probably just a dolphin. Or a trick of the light,' he said. 'And as for it not being safe to swim . . . Do you really think anyone's going to swim in *that*?'

The man looked at the beach. The officer had a point. Last night's cool yellow sand had been replaced by sticky black sludge. The white-peaked waves weren't crashing to the shore, they were oozing in and breaking in a gloopy mess. The sea was oily black.

'This is the busiest holiday month of the year. And yesterday,' reminded the policeman, 'that was one of the cleanest beaches in the country. Today there's enough oil on it to fry chips.'

Both men stared at the scene. There were no tourists on the beach; instead it was populated with news reporters all desperate to get a new angle on the Toxic Terror.

'So here we are on Haven Beach,' began one reporter, talking straight to a camera. 'As you

The Haven Eye

TOXIC TERROR SWEEPS BRITAIN'S SEASIDES

can see, the pictures tell a tale of environmental disaster. Nobody knows where the oil came from, but what we do know is that yesterday this was a Blue Flag beach, one of the cleanest in the country. And now it's, well . . .' she said, pausing for effect, 'it's been black flagged. There won't be any tourists in *this* town for the summer season.' She gave a grim smile to the camera. 'Here with me I have one of the country's leading environmental experts,

Professor Axon.' She turned to the woman beside her. 'Professor, tell us about the so-called "Toxic Terror",' the reporter said. 'Have the authorities got any clues as to who's behind these environmental crimes?'

'Toxic Terror indeed,' the professor said. 'As you know, this disaster is just another in a series of ecological mishaps that have taken place along Britain's coast. As you've reported in the past month, every single oil disaster has been on a Blue Flag beach. It seems the culprit is wiping out the very cleanest parts of the British coastline one by one. Hardly any of these beaches remain.'

The reporter nodded, looking serious, as she turned back to the camera. 'As we heard earlier,' she said, building up for a big finale, 'there are now only three Blue Flag beaches left. It seems the many sea birds and fish that have suffered from this oil aren't the only endangered species. The traditional seaside holiday may soon become a thing of the past.'

3. Top Dog

Lara and her two pups Spud and Star had spent a day with *their* leading expert, Professor Maximus Cortex. The professor was one of the world's top scientists, and the brains behind the British government's animal spying programme. He knew a top dog when he saw one.

The scientist looked down at his clipboard and then peered over his spectacles at the puppies. He addressed the black and white puppy first, his face breaking into a warm smile. 'Good work, Agent Star,' he smiled. 'Your fitness levels are top-notch. Dare I say, you're even fitter than your mother was at this stage of her training.'

Star sat proudly, her neck stretched with pride. Her mum nodded approvingly.

Her brother sat beside her, his tail swishing, more in hope than expectation. Professor Cortex turned his attention to the black puppy. The angle of his eyebrow told Spud all he needed to know. 'That's worse than last week, young pup,' he noted. 'Your fitness levels leave a lot to be desired.'

Spud sat, his head hanging in shame, his tongue hanging from the side of his mouth. He tried to hold his tummy in a bit. *Sorry, Prof*, he wagged. *But this frame's not built for speed. I'm more of an ideas dog. You know, a problem-solver, a thinker, creative solutions, an IT specialist. Good with gadgets. That kind of thing. If you want speed and fitness*, he nodded towards his sister, *that's her game.*

Star was a sleek black and white fitness machine. She had completed the three-mile run in record time and, what's more, she wasn't even panting. Spud loved his sister, but it was frustrating that she was so fit and bouncy.

'If you want to qualify as a Spy Dog, you will have to improve, Spud,' warned the professor. 'Tomorrow is your big day. The pair of you will be completing the SAS assault course, against *real* soldiers. These are the fittest, meanest and toughest that this country has to offer. And you have to keep up with them. Got it?'

Star wagged enthusiastically. *Got it, Prof. Bring it on!* 'Come on, bro,' she woofed. 'Let's be positive. If we work together, we can rise to the challenge. This time tomorrow we are going to qualify as fully fledged Spy Dogs – just like Ma!'

Spud nodded. It was all he'd ever wanted, to follow in his mum's footsteps and graduate as a proper Spy Dog. Spud's ambition was to go on a real mission. Sure, he and his sister had had a couple of accidental adventures. *But I want at least one proper, 100% dangerous James Bond-style mission.*

Their mum nodded in encouragement. Even

though she was retired now, as the world's first-ever Spy Dog she knew what it took to pass the fitness test. Lara thought back to her Spy School days. *In those days I was code name GM451*, she thought proudly. *My real name came from the initials Licensed Assault and Rescue Animal, the first graduate of the professor's Spy School. Top of the class by a mile*, she smiled. Lara liked to think that the puppies had inherited her strengths. Star had her speed and endurance. *She can run forever!* Lara remembered back to her crime-fighting adventures. *With all those baddies I captured, physical fitness was crucial*. And what Spud lacked in fitness he made up for in brains. Between them, they were the perfect team.

There was more than enough action and adventure, she remembered, putting her paw to her sticky-up ear. *This bullet hole is a reminder!* Lara shuddered as she remembered her close encounter with Mr Big, an evil villain who had tried to kill her several times. *Too close for comfort! Mr Big was the evilest baddie imaginable*. She thought back to a recent adventure and breathed a sigh of relief. *That aeroplane accident means he's gone for good!*

Since Lara had been allowed to retire from

active service, she'd concentrated on being a normal family pet. *Except life is far from 'normal'. All I want to do is be a mum. And keep the puppies safe from harm.* But Lara knew that she could never truly relax. Because of her past there might always be baddies trying to seek revenge on her. Professor Cortex had advised her to make sure the puppies were up to speed with the latest gadgets and spying techniques. 'You never know when enemy agents from the past might attack again,' he'd warned. And unfortunately Mr Big was just one of many people she'd put behind bars.

So Lara had agreed to put Spud and Star through their paces. She was certain that they'd never leave home and go on deadly missions. *But there seems to be enough adventure in the neighbourhood to keep them occupied*, she sighed. *Peace and quiet? Not a chance!*

The Cook family's people carrier pulled up and the children jumped out. Lara had lived with the Cooks since they adopted her from the RSPCA a few years ago, not knowing she was a Spy Dog. But they got suspicious when she started surfing the Internet and practising her karate moves in the back yard. Eventually her secret identity had to be revealed, and so the family had been close to Professor Cortex ever since.

Sophie was first through the door today, throwing her arms around Spud's chubby frame. 'How did it go, little fella?' she asked. 'Did you pass the fitness test?'

Spud's ears flopped and his belly drooped. 'Not great,' he yapped. *Perhaps I need to stay off the donuts for a while?*

The Cooks' youngest, Ollie, charged in next and made a beeline for Star. 'Top of the class?' he asked. Star sat proudly, her wag giving away her super result.

Ben strolled in last. He was the oldest and the coolest of the children. He and Lara had a special bond and often spent time together, fishing at the lake, riding their bikes or camping in the rain. He patted his dog on the head and she looked up adoringly.

Being a family pet is just the best thing ever! she wagged.

'Mum's waiting in the car today,' said Sophie. 'She said something about she'd "rather not know" when I asked if she wanted to see the latest gadgets.'

Professor Cortex blushed. He was used to being in trouble with Mrs Cook when the children and pups accidentally got into danger. 'OK . . . yes, well, we're all present and correct then.' He winked at the children and excited dogs. 'And have I got some gadgets for you!'

Professor Cortex lived for his work. He loved Lara and he'd grown very fond of the children too. Ben, Sophie and Ollie had got used to the professor's frantic arm-waving – they realized this was just his sheer enthusiasm for Spy School, and especially his inventions. Some of his gadgets were brilliant and others totally useless. On the brilliant side he'd invented satnav dog collars, and a rocket-powered skateboard for George the tortoise. On the downside he'd invented an automatic haircutter that had totally embarrassed Dad. Last time they were at Spy School the professor had shown them his latest invention – a torch that worked in the daylight.

Ben had scratched his head in puzzlement. 'Not sure about that one, Prof,' he'd admitted. 'I mean, what's the point?'

The professor had looked a little disappointed.

'I see what you mean,' he'd agreed. 'Maybe it's an idea that's ahead of its time.'

'Or an idea that's so rubbish its time will never come,' whispered Sophie to her brother.

As they waited to see the new gadgets, the children and dogs looked at the professor. As always, he was dressed in a white lab coat, his spectacles halfway down his nose. He bent down and addressed the puppies, his eyes twinkling with excitement. 'I have a couple of inventions I want you to know about. Firstly, and this is the grooviest thing ever,' said the professor, trying to sound cool, 'check out these.' Professor Cortex pulled a small tin from his pocket and rattled it. 'This will change the world. Follow me, everyone.'

4. O24U

The children and dogs trotted behind obediently as the professor strode out of the room and along one of the many long white corridors that made up Spy School. The professor didn't do 'slow' so Ollie had to jog to keep up. Spud and Star's paws tapped on the tiled floor. They turned left, then right, then right again before the scientist came to a door marked *Swimming Pool*. Lara sniffed. She could smell the chlorine.

Professor Cortex put his eye to the identity machine and it scanned his iris. The door swished open and the professor ushered them in.

'Cool,' said Ollie, 'are we going for a swim?'

An Olympic-sized swimming pool lay before them, its surface perfectly smooth.

'What you're about to see is absolutely top

secret,' said the professor, taking off his coat and undoing his shirt.

Yikes, thought Star as the old man revealed his hairy chest. *Don't worry, I won't be telling anyone about that!*

Next, off came his trousers and socks until the professor stood before them in just his Union Jack swimming trunks, which he had put on underneath in preparation for his demonstration.

Not very cool, thought Lara, eyeing his trunks. *No wonder you want to keep them secret.*

'Now, time for the invention,' said the professor. He took the small tin from his coat pocket and opened the lid. The children peered inside.

'Oooh, marbles,' smiled Ollie. 'Can I play?'

Spud wagged enthusiastically. *Me too, Prof.*

'Aha, young Oliver!' beamed the professor. 'Tricked you. They are not marbles, they are oxygen pills. For breathing underwater.'

Wow, thought Lara. *That's amazing. I could have used those a few times when I was a Spy Dog. If they work, that is!*

'Still experimental,' admitted the professor, taking a red 'marble' and popping it into his mouth. 'But each capsule should provide approximately three minutes of oxygen,' he said, rolling the capsule around his mouth before swallowing with a big gulp. 'Allow me to demonstrate.'

The old man quickly replaced his glasses with special goggles, then turned and walked to the edge of the pool. He raised his arms above his head and pointed his fingers like he'd seen Olympic swimmers do. And then he belly-flopped his pale body into the pool. There was a slap as his tummy hit the water, and the children and dogs approached the edge of the pool to get a closer look. The professor was at the deep end, sitting on the bottom of the pool. He looked up through the water and saw rippled faces looking down. He waved and the children waved back.

A minute passed. 'He's been down there an awfully long time,' said Sophie.

'But he's waving again,' said Ollie, 'so he must be OK.'

The seconds ticked by. 'Here he comes,' woofed Spud as the professor swam up to the surface. His bald head appeared and he puffed out his cheeks before gulping fresh oxygen. He grinned at the onlookers. He held his wrist to the surface and tapped his watch. 'Three minutes and forty-two seconds,' he spluttered. 'And I could have done more!'

Ben helped the professor out of the pool.

'So, what do you think?' he asked excitedly, wiping water from his face.

'Amazing!' admitted Ollie.

'Thank you, young Oliver,' beamed the professor. 'The pills react with the body's white blood cells to produce oxygen, you see. So, instead of having to breathe you just hold your nose and let your body produce enough oxygen to keep you going. These are low strength. I'm working on a super-strength version that will allow people to stay underwater for hours, maybe even days.'

'Yuck,' groaned Ollie, 'you'd be all wrinkly.'

'I'm marketing them as "O24U",' grinned the professor.

Very clever, thought Spud.

'I don't get it,' Ollie piped up.

'O_2 is the chemical symbol for oxygen,' explained Sophie. 'Geddit? Oxygen . . . for you?'

Ollie shrugged his shoulders. 'I think you should call them "fishfood". That's better. Then I'd buy them.'

And what about dogs? thought Lara. *Do they work on animals, Prof?* she wondered.

Professor Cortex knew exactly what she was thinking. 'And the very good news is that they absolutely do work on animals, GM451,' he nodded. The professor bent down and clipped a small pouch on to Star's collar. 'One for you,' he said, putting an O24U pill into the pouch. 'And one for you, Agent Spud,' he added, as the puppy almost wagged himself off his feet. 'Emergencies only.'

'Thanks, Prof,' woofed Spud. *I hope I get an opportunity to try my new gadget!* he thought to himself.

The children and dogs returned to the professor's lab and waited while he dried off and got dressed. It wasn't long before he bounded back into the lab. 'And just one more invention,' he beamed. 'Who wants it?'

Ollie's hand was up first. 'But you don't even know what it is, Master Oliver,' chuckled the scientist. 'Here you go.' He tossed a small black object to the youngest child. 'It's a super-magnet. Obviously, I'll be calling it a "mega-mag" when it hits the shops. It's a normal magnet, so sticks to metal objects. Until, that is, you press the red button on the side. Then it will massively increase the magnetism of whatever it's attached to.'

Ollie looked puzzled.

'What do we need a giant magnet for, Prof?' barked Star.

Professor Cortex could see the confusion on everyone's faces. 'Here,' he said, 'allow me to demonstrate.'

Ollie handed the gadget back. The scientist

21

looked around for something metal. 'See this chair?' he said. 'The magnet will stick to the metal frame . . . like so . . . and when I press this little red button the whole chair becomes magnetized.' The professor pressed the button. Nothing happened. The children looked at each other and shrugged. 'Now, young Oliver, go over to my tool-box and open it.'

Ollie wandered over to the professor's tool-box and unclipped the lid. 'And everyone prepare to duck,' warned the professor.

Ollie pulled back the lid and there was a clank of metal as the spanners, screws and bolts hurled themselves out of the box and shot towards the magnetic chair. It was all over in three seconds. Everyone stared at the chair, which had almost disappeared under a weight of metal objects.

The professor smiled. 'Not quite sure what the use is yet,' he admitted. 'But it's really great fun! Next time you come, I'll have that worked out. Now, home-time before Mrs Cook thinks

I've got you all into another scrape. The pups need to rest before their big day tomorrow.'

Mum drove the dogs and children home from Spy School. She turned on the radio and sighed at the news report. 'Have you heard?' she shouted to the children in the back. 'Another beach has been wiped out.'

'No way,' protested Sophie. 'All those poor fish and birds!'

'Not to mention the hotel owners and all those who rely on tourism,' agreed Ben. 'It's an environmental disaster.'

'We've gone from dozens of clean Blue Flag beaches to just three,' said Mum, navigating the car round a roundabout. 'Luckily for us, we're booked in at Pleasure Island Resort, which is one of the clean ones. Touch wood,' she said, tapping Spud's head, 'the "Toxic Terror" will steer clear and we'll enjoy a fabulously sunny holiday on a beautiful clean island.'

Lara crossed her paws. *A relaxing holiday is just what we all need. I can't wait to teach the pups how to water-ski.*

Ben, Sophie and Ollie looked at each other.

They were looking forward to sun and sand, not an environmental emergency. Each raised their hands and crossed their fingers.

5. Toxic Terror

The local residents sat in the town hall. Camera crews were positioned at the back of the room. There was a general air of gloominess. The residents chattered away to each other, complaining about what they'd heard on the news.

Eventually a senior policewoman stood on stage and the crowd hushed. 'Thank you, ladies and gentlemen,' she began. 'I'd like to extend a warm welcome to the residents of the three remaining Blue Flag beaches in Britain – Pleasure Island,' she said, looking to her left, 'and Blue Bay and Sandy Shore,' she said, looking to the audience on her right.

'We don't want a warm welcome,' shouted an angry voice. 'We want to know what you're doing about the Toxic Terror.'

'Yes,' shouted another annoyed voice. 'What are the police doing to save our beaches from pollution? And our livelihoods?'

Other people joined in the shouting and the policewoman had to wait a minute to speak again. 'This emergency meeting is to let you know that we're doing everything we can to protect your coastline. As you know, this seems to be a systematic attack on the cleanest beaches in Britain. Logic tells us that the attacker — whoever he or she is — will target your towns next.'

She waited while the uproar calmed down.

'We don't know where the oil is coming from. Or how it's being pumped on to the beaches,' she admitted. 'Based on the other beaches, we now know it's not being washed ashore. This is a calculated spill. So we're patrolling the coastline in case it's coming by ship in the dead of night. And we've set up road blocks in case it's coming by tanker. Whoever is behind the poisoning is clearly very evil . . .'

'Or very clever,' piped up an elderly gentleman at the back. 'This Toxic Terror seems to have outwitted the police for months. I'm the owner of Pleasure Island Resort. My life savings have gone into this island.' There was a gentle murmuring of agreement from the residents before the old man continued. 'Surely by now you've got more clues?'

'Nothing,' admitted the policewoman. 'But you can be sure that we will eventually catch this evil villain,' she lied. 'And when we do, they will feel the full force of the law.'

The meeting broke up and the residents grumbled their way home. The old man stayed behind to chat to the police officer. 'This evil baddie is turning out to be more of a creative genius, outsmarting you lot,' he suggested.

The policewoman rolled her eyes in frustration. 'Look here, sir,' she replied. 'Dozens of the country's best beaches have been ruined. The ocean polluted. Sea-life killed. Tourism blighted. Coastal towns devastated. Creative genius?' she laughed. '*Evil* genius is closer to the mark. Now, if you'll excuse me,' she huffed, and walked away.

The old man smiled to himself, then shuffled out of the town hall to his car. His blacked-out windows meant nobody could see him as he clicked the doors locked and turned the rear-view mirror to see his reflection. It really did pain him to smile. His scarred hand went to his face and he felt the deep wrinkles. 'Evil genius,' he said, letting the phrase sink in. 'She says I'm an evil genius.'

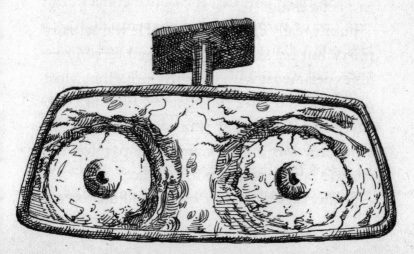

The old man popped out his contact lenses and his red eyes stared back. 'I may look ninety years old,' he cackled to himself, 'but it's been worth it.' Jimmy thought back to his last adventure. His evil plan to shoot a hole in the ozone layer had gone horribly wrong. 'That blasted mutt,' he cursed, staring into his red-eyed reflection. 'Spy Dog,' he spat. 'And her father! I hope they're both *dead* dogs!

'But this new scheme is working out brilliantly. Nobody will suspect that frail old Jimmy, the owner of Pleasure Island Resort, is really the Toxic Terror. When Pleasure Island is the only clean beach left, I'll be able to raise my prices and charge whatever I want, just like any good businessman would. Little old Jimmy will soon be a multi-billionaire and no one will suspect a thing.'

Jimmy really did look ninety. He was actually thirty but his skin had been aged terribly by his experiments with the sun's radiation. Most people would have thought it a high price to pay. But for Jimmy it was worth it. After all, when he was a billionaire he'd pay for the world's best surgeon to fix his face.

Jimmy turned the key and the engine roared.

He pulled out into the traffic and set off back to Pleasure Island. 'Two more beaches to go,' he grinned. 'Then my resort will be the *only* place to visit.' Jimmy's wrinkled face attempted another smile. 'And as for the final beach. I think I'll finish it off in style.'

6. Star Jumps

The Cook family and Professor Cortex were waiting anxiously while the puppies completed their warm-up routine. Lara was putting them through their paces. Around them, Britain's finest military personnel were also warming

BLANK
FIRE
ONLY
MOD

up. They were dressed in full combat gear, with backpacks and heavy boots. An assault course stretched before them.

Spud's tummy was touching the ground as he did his press-ups. And as he watched his sister, he figured 'Star Jumps' were named after her. He huffed and puffed his way through his mum's instructions, almost worn out before the assault course began! In the distance he could see huge fences, water jumps, barbed wire and ditches full of water.

'*I* did it,' said Lara, giving her best pep-talk, 'and the Prof says you can't graduate to fully fledged "Spy Dog" status unless you

complete the course in under thirty minutes. OK?'

'Yes, Mum!' barked Star, jogging on the spot.

'Er, yes, Ma,' woofed Spud, ears drooping. 'I'll do my best.'

'Teamwork,' reminded Lara. 'Some of the barriers require speed of paw,' she said, casting an eye at Star, 'and some speed of thought,' she said, smiling at Spud. 'And all the obstacles require effort and bravery.'

'And what about these soldiers?' woofed Star. 'Do we need to beat them?'

'No,' said Lara. 'These guys and girls are the best of the best from the Army, Navy and Air Force. You're all against the clock, that's all. Finish in less than thirty minutes, that's the goal.'

'I don't think he likes us,' said Star, glancing at one of the competitors.

Spud looked up and the man shook a fist at the puppies. 'I hate dogs,' he mouthed.

Lara looked at his uniform and name tag. 'He's Lieutenant Black, from the Navy,' she woofed, glaring at the man. 'Try not to let him put you off. These people are very competitive.

They'd absolutely hate to be beaten by a canine!'

'We'll do our best, Mum,' yapped Star, bouncing from side to side with excitement. 'Let us at 'em!'

Spud looked over to the start line as the SAS commander, a huge man with bulging arms, stood at the front. 'Competitors ready?' he bellowed.

'As I'll ever be,' whined Spud under his breath. 'Remind me to keep away from Black, though!'

The commander put a whistle to his lips and they were away. Thirty minutes and counting . . .

Jimmy approached Pleasure Island Resort and marvelled at his achievement. A gleaming hotel stood in the middle of the island. '*My* island!' he said as he drove across the bridge. There was an indoor ski dome, amusement arcades, shops, cafes and, best of all, the bluest sky, most golden sand and cleanest beach in the country. Pleasure Island Resort was booked solid for the next twelve months. He'd doubled his prices but bookings kept rolling in — thanks to the Toxic Terror!

'And soon I'll be doubling prices again,' he sneered as he pulled his car in to a small bungalow on the island, with a *PRIVATE PROPERTY* sign outside. He pressed a button on the dashboard and the garage doors hummed open, and then shut once he was inside. Jimmy liked people to think that he lived in a normal house, just like all the visitors who came to spend their money on Pleasure Island. But once inside the garage, he pressed the button again and his car started the journey downwards to his underground bunker.

7. Water Puppy

Spud made it through the first part of the course. Star helped him over a high wall and, in turn, he gave her a leg up a rope-ladder. Climbing wasn't their strongest talent, and things were made worse as the dog-hating Lieutenant Black barged past and nearly knocked Spud off the ladder.

'Careful,' yapped the pup. 'I could have been hurt!' Instead of apologizing, Spud thought he saw the man smile. Next, the puppies had to cross a wobbly rope-bridge. The horrible man deliberately wobbled the bridge as the puppies were halfway across, causing Star to fall and have to start again. Lieutenant Black waved as she fell. 'See you later, mutt,' he sneered. 'There's no way a dog will ever beat me!'

By the course's halfway point, Spud was

struggling. His chest was heaving and his doggy limbs aching. He'd just tummy-crawled under some barbed wire and had cut himself. He stopped for a breather and to lick his wound while his sister bounded ahead.

Before long Star was back, woofing excitedly. 'Quickly, bro,' she panted, 'there's trouble ahead. Someone's in a major bother! C'mon, we might be able to help.'

Spud had a stitch but his sister sounded serious so he sprinted for all he was worth. 'In there,' she barked, pointing to a watery ditch. 'This is the next obstacle. It's an underwater pipe that we have to swim through . . . but someone's stuck, halfway!'

'*Yikes!*' yapped Spud. 'I'm the best swimmer, let me take a look.' The brave puppy launched himself into the water and paddled forward, his stumpy legs pumping hard. Then he took a deep breath and disappeared.

Star watched a few bubbles popping on the surface, then nothing.

Spud was swimming as if his life depended on it. *Maybe it does*, he thought. *Better be careful not to get stuck too*. The water was cold and murky so he couldn't see very far ahead. He found the entrance to the pipe and in he went. Spud's lungs began to hurt — all that leg work was using up his oxygen supply. He came to a blockage in the tunnel. *Star's right*, he thought, *it's a soldier. But not just any soldier — it's that horrible one who shook us off the bridge!*

The lieutenant was flapping about, his eyes wild with panic. Through the murk, Spud could see the man's backpack was caught on a nail. The puppy tried to free the panic-stricken man but it was no use. *No time to get back for another gulp of air*, thought Spud, his brain getting dizzy. *There's only one solution!* Spud fumbled for the pouch on his collar. He pressed the button and it sprang open. *This is the risky bit*, he thought. The red O24U pill floated by

and Spud caught it between his paws. By now the man had stopped struggling. He was closer to dead than alive. Spud felt for the man's mouth with his paws. He forced open the lieutenant's mouth and inserted the pill. *Swallow, man, swallow*, thought the frantic puppy. *I've got to leave you now.*

Spud's tiny legs pumped and he glided through the muddy water. His legs were heavy and he felt strangely light-headed.

Star was standing by the side of the ditch, waiting. *Come on, bro, you can do it!* Through the muddy water she could see Spud's legs were moving slowly as he paddled, then they stopped altogether as he reached the surface. Leaning in, she caught him by his collar and hauled him on to the grass. She wasn't even sure if he was alive.

Star remembered her dog first-aid training – she lay Spud on his tummy and jumped up and down on his back. On the third jump a stream of muddy water gushed out of his mouth and he gasped for air.

She saw Lieutenant Black emerge from the other end of the water tunnel. *Not him!*

The man spluttered and coughed up some

water. He looked over at the puppies and rubbed his eyes in disbelief, then got to his feet and jogged over to them. 'Are you OK, little fella?' he asked Spud. 'I'm not sure what you fed me but I owe you my life!'

'We're OK,' coughed Spud. 'I think?'

Star nodded. 'And as for life saving . . . all in a day's work for a Spy Pup. Hopefully you won't wobble us off any more bridges now!'

The man scooped up Spud and tucked him into his backpack. Then he checked his watch and away he jogged, Star bounding by his side.

Five minutes and counting! Black thought to himself. His lucky escape meant his adrenalin was pumping, so he covered the last mile in almost record time. The digital clock on the finishing line was in sight.

'Come on, Lieutenant,' yelped Spud, bouncing up and down in the backpack. 'Twelve seconds to go!'

The naval officer had given his all. Star ran ahead and finished well within the limit. 'Yessss,' she woofed. 'I've done it. I qualify as a Spy Dog!'

Lieutenant Black staggered towards the line. The digital numbers clicked down – 4, 3, 2 –

and he collapsed over the line, sending Spud tumbling from the backpack. 'Yes!' yelped the puppy. 'Finished with one second to go . . . *and* I saved someone's life along the way.' Spud hugged his sister.

Lara, the professor and the Cook family cheered as the SAS commander approached the puppies. They sat, tails swishing, doggy grins on their faces. The commander bent down and shook Star's paw. 'Congratulations, young dog,' he said, placing a medal around her neck.

Star's neck lengthened with pride. *Look, Ma,* she wagged. *I've passed! I'm a Spy Dog, like you!*

The commander turned to Spud and his face fell. 'But you, young dog,' he said, 'have failed the test.'

Spud looked shocked. His tail stopped swishing and his face drooped. *But*, he thought, *I made it with a second to go?*

'You cheated,' bellowed the commander. 'You hitched a lift with Lieutenant Black here,' he said, pointing to the collapsed man. 'And the British SAS does not reward cheats!'

'Excuse *me*,' argued Professor Cortex, 'but these puppies are not cheats. I'm sure there's a perfectly reasonable explanation . . .'

The lieutenant raised himself off the ground. 'But, Sarge,' he began, 'the little dog —'

'And you've failed as well, Lieutenant Black,' snarled his commanding officer, ignoring the professor. 'Aiding and abetting a mutt indeed.'

'Are you crazy, mister?' barked Star. 'You didn't see what my bro did to save his life!' She ran over to her mum. 'Spud is a superhero!'

Spud's doggy jowls fell further as he realized that his dream was over. He ran to Star and Lara and buried his face in his mum's tummy.

'All I want is to be a proper Spy Dog,' he sobbed. 'And carry out a real mission. Just one real mission. It's not fair, Ma!'

Lara stroked Spud's ears. 'You've done well, son,' she soothed. 'You saved the man's life. I'm proud of you. Your time for a real mission will come sooner than you think.'

8. Cave Man

Jimmy parked his car and got out. He was glad to be home. 'OK, so it's not a normal "home",' he said to himself, 'but then I'm not a normal person. I'm a creative genius, inventor and soon-to-be billionaire!'

The underground cavern was huge. He'd modelled it on the Batcave he'd seen in a movie. In fact, Jimmy liked the whole Batman idea. The secrecy, the outfit, the superhero, the cool car and the darkness of a cave. Jimmy's skin condition meant that exposure to sunlight was rather painful, so it suited him to be underground.

Jimmy was a little disappointed that the press had labelled him the 'Toxic Terror'. 'But it's a brilliant business strategy,' he reminded himself. 'I should be winning awards for my creative thinking. Not being hunted like a dog.' Jimmy knew there was a fine line between genius and insanity, but he was sure he was on the right side of that line. His brain was the best in the business!

He looked in the mirror and imagined he was on a chat show. 'Thank you, thank you.' He smiled to the imaginary audience. He practised his wave to the camera. The mirror image looked wrinkled and haggard but Jimmy

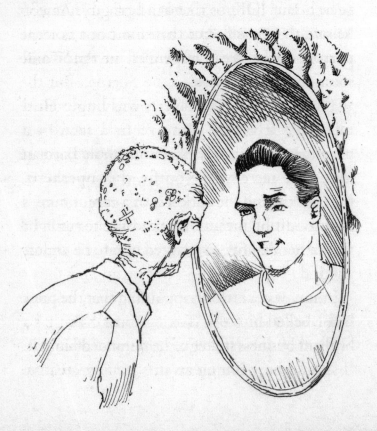

imagined the chat shows would happen *after* his planned surgery. He pictured a film star with twinkling eyes and smooth complexion. *And pearly white teeth*, he thought.

Jimmy raised an eyebrow and smiled at the imaginary host. 'Yes, Jonathan,' he chuckled, 'you are lucky to have me on your show . . . The secret of my success? Oh, Jonathan,' he grinned at the mirror. 'You know, lots of wildly successful people keep their strategy secret. But I'm not that kind of guy. As you know, the press used to make me out as some sort of evil baddie. They called me the "Toxic Terror",' he chuckled to the mirror. 'But the plan was always very clear. Firstly, to pollute all the other beaches so that Pleasure Island was the only clean beach in the country and I could rake in money from desperate holiday-makers. But of course – and here's the genius bit – I wanted to help clean up the beaches that I'd polluted. I'm a good guy, remember?' Jimmy did his eyebrow thing once again and shot a glance sideways at a second imaginary camera. *That would win people over*, he thought.

'So the other half of my plan was, of course, to be part of the clean-up. You see, I have another company called Calamity Clean-up – such a fun name – that is the country's biggest environmental cleansing business. So, you see, I didn't want to do lasting damage. Just temporary wipe-out.' He imagined the studio audience breaking into spontaneous applause at this generous act. 'All the towns that I've polluted will be hiring me to clean up their act.' Jimmy slapped his knee. 'Total genius. And think how many jobs I've created,' he smiled. 'All those people cleaning up the oil, all those volunteers washing oil off birds, all those camera crews and reporters. It's a boom time!' Jimmy's mobile rang and he was brought back to reality.

'Yes?' he barked. 'OK,' he said, 'come on down.' He pushed a button on the lift, which started to move.

Jimmy looked around his cavern. His living quarters were to his right. Bedroom, bathroom, kitchen. Plus his office, the nerve-centre of his business empire. Several laptops twinkled away. A bank of TV screens beamed life on Pleasure Island into his office. Jimmy had every centimetre of the island covered. He loved watching his customers spend their hard-earned cash.

To his left was a huge pool of water, leading to a twisting passage and secret opening at the base of the island's many cliffs. A large *DANGER! ROCKS FALLING* sign on the cliff face kept nosy holiday-makers from exploring the cave. 'Just me and my . . . er . . . submarine,' he murmured, walking towards the edge of the pool. A huge black submarine sat in the water, awaiting its next poisonous mission. Jimmy had painted huge eyes and sharp-looking teeth on the front, so it had become a terrifying metal monster. He jumped on to the submarine and shook his fists like a Premiership footballer who'd just scored the winning goal. 'It's the perfect plan,' he yelled. 'Just two more beaches to pollute!'

The lift started beeping and an oil tanker was lowered into the cavern. The lorry door was pushed open and a metal foot swung out. Jimmy always marvelled at new technology, and this foot, and the leg that followed, were amazing. He'd seen sci-fi movies where robots had taken over the world, so this fitted into his plans perfectly.

The lorry driver jumped down from the cab, his metal foot sparking on the cave floor. The driver did what he always did first – struck a match and lit a huge cigar, purple smoke filling the cavern.

'Good morning, Mr Big.' Jimmy smiled. 'Glad you could make it.'

9. A Big Plan

<u>Three months ago</u>

*Mr Big had always hated dogs. But right now, he
had even more reason to dislike them. He'd poisoned
Lara, or GM451 as the mad professor called her.
And he'd trapped her stupid puppies in an aeroplane.
And then he'd jumped . . . with a parachute, of
course. Except when he pulled the ripcord he discovered
it wasn't a parachute at all. It was one of those pesky
kids' backpacks. Some cheese and onion crisps and a
tuna sandwich floated past him and he gulped. Not
good!*

*Mr Big had had nearly a minute to think about
things on the way down. His cheeks flapped and his
eyes watered as he hurtled to earth. But luck was on his
side. There was a lake below and he hit the water with
an almighty splash. It must have been the world's
biggest-ever belly-flop. Boy, did it sting! He remembered*

51

there was a lot of writhing about in the lake as he struggled to free himself from the backpack. And lots of pain. There had been some fish. Then his memory went patchy. He'd hauled himself on to the bank – which is difficult when you're half-drowned and your body is broken in lots of places. He lay on the bank of the lake and marvelled that he was alive. He looked down and saw his leg was missing. His ears were ringing and his vision blurred. Mr Big put his hand to his left eye and felt an empty socket. His right eye saw his left eye, bobbing in the lake. He remembered feeling for his cigars but they were too wet to light. He remembered that this upset him more than losing his leg.

But Mr Big was a fighter. OK, so I've lost a leg, he'd thought. And an eye. And some teeth. And some of my good looks. But I've still got my beautiful criminal brain. Then he'd dragged

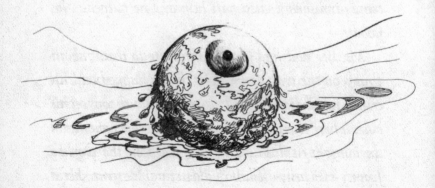

himself into some bushes and drifted into dreamland.

Mr Big had been woken by a police helicopter hovering above the lake. Frogmen were entering the water, searching for his body. One of the men had scooped his eye up in a net. The evil villain could hear police dogs barking and knew they'd soon be sniffing around the bushes. He remembered feeling for his mobile and being pleased that it was in working order. He flicked through his contacts, wondering who to call.

Who can I trust in my moment of need?

His eye focused for just a second and he saw a name: Jimmy.

Perfect! Mr Big smiled through his agonizing pain. He and Jimmy went back a long way. They'd met in prison many years ago, even sharing a cell. Jimmy was a small man, easily bullied by the other inmates, but Mr Big had protected him. As he lay there in the bushes he figured it was time to call in the favour.

The call was made and Jimmy had arranged an emergency private helicopter to collect his partner-in-crime immediately and take him to a top-secret hospital where no one would ask questions about his terrible injuries. Then Mr Big had sought refuge at Jimmy's Pleasure Island hideaway to recover. He'd *been rebuilt. His bionic leg worked a treat. His eye-patch masked the hole. Gold teeth soon filled the gaps in his mouth.*

There's a saying that two heads are better than one. And the two most evil heads on the planet had teamed up once again, for the world's most dangerous environmental plan. The world could forget Pleasure Island . . . this was 100% Danger Island.

10. Checking In

'One lorry-load of heavy engine oil, as requested,' said Mr Big, snarling in the dim light of the cave.

'Well, let's not delay any longer,' cheered Jimmy. 'Let's load her up and get polluting!'

Mr Big stomped his way to the lorry hose. He pulled at it and walked over to the submarine, the pipe extending behind him. He undid a cap on the side of the sub and fixed the hose in place. He gave the thumbs-up and Jimmy, standing at the lorry, turned on a tap. There was a glugging noise as the oil was pumped into a tank on the submarine. After five minutes the deadly transfer was complete.

'Job done,' said Mr Big, unhooking the tube. 'Toxic cargo fully loaded.'

Jimmy smiled as far as his damaged face would

let him. 'Tonight's the night,' he said, rubbing his hands with glee. 'We'll pollute another resort. And then do you know what, Big? I think we'll arrange something extra-evil for the very last beach.'

Mr Big looked interested. Of all four-letter words, 'evil' was his favourite. 'Such as?' he asked.

'How about a real statement?' suggested Jimmy. 'Oil pollution is great fun. But what about something more . . . permanent?'

'Like what?' purred Mr Big.

'What about *nuclear* waste?' smiled Jimmy. 'That should leave a lasting glow!'

Mr Big snarled his biggest grin of the month. 'I love it,' he purred, 'when a plan goes from bad to evil!'

The Cooks checked into their apartment at Pleasure Island Resort. Professor Cortex was booked in at the apartment next door. As a rule he didn't do holidays, but Lara had persuaded him that he deserved a week off. She'd watched him pack his suitcase. One white lab coat, one pair of trousers, one pair of clean pants and forty-five science books.

'An opportunity to relax,' he smiled at Lara.

'It's so cool that dogs are allowed here,' woofed Star. 'This is going to be the best holiday ever.'

Spud wasn't so sure. He was still sulking from yesterday's assault course. 'No missions though,' he grumbled, 'because Mr Failure's not allowed!'

'Cheer up, son,' yapped Lara. 'Stop feeling sorry for yourself. You can always re-take the test. And besides, this is a holiday, not a mission. Just ask Mrs C,' she barked, casting a glance at Mum. 'I think you'll find adventure is off limits!'

Spud knew she was right. Mrs Cook

wouldn't let them go anywhere near danger. They'd accidentally got into a few scrapes in the last few months and Mrs Cook had issued a warning to the professor, the children and the dogs. 'You are *not* superheroes,' she'd warned, wagging a finger around the room. 'You lot are *not* the Famous Five,' she said, aiming her finger at the children. 'You are *not* Scooby-Doo,' she said, turning her attention to the dogs. 'And you, sir, the worst of them all,' she bellowed at Professor Cortex, 'are *not* Doctor Who. We are a *normal* family. With *normal* pets. And for once,' she warned, 'we are going to have a *normal* holiday. Understood?'

Mum's talks were always pretty clear. There had been a lot of looking down at shoes and paws. Dogs and people had nodded. 'Yes, Mum,' the children had mumbled.

Now, here they stood, on their very own Pleasure Island holiday. 'We've seen it on the telly,' said Ollie. 'And now we're actually here. It's going to be brilliant!'

'It's bloomin' expensive,' grumbled Dad. 'In fact it's a rip-off.'

'But look at the clean beach,' reminded Sophie. 'No oil in sight!'

'And great weather,' reminded Mum. 'Pleasure Island has its own micro-climate, remember. Sunny all year round. So we don't mind paying a bit extra,' she suggested.

'A bit!' mumbled Dad. 'I hope you lot aren't banking on drinking or eating much. Have you seen the prices in the restaurant?'

'But eating and drinking is an essential part of the holiday, Mr C,' yapped Spud, thinking of his tummy.

'I vote we go and explore,' said Star. 'Who's coming with me?' she woofed, pawing at the door.

Lara followed, standing on her hind legs and opening the door. 'Come on, kids, let's go and see what Pleasure Island has to offer.'

Sandy Shore was on full alert. The residents were twitchy. They knew there were only three Blue Flag beaches left. Police had set up road-blocks to make sure no oil tankers could get through. Navy warships patrolled the coastline to stop any ships coming close. In their wildest imaginations, nobody had considered that the Toxic Terror would be delivering his nasty cargo from a submarine.

Jimmy loved his submarine. He'd watched lots of films and always wore a captain's hat like they did in the movies. He checked the time. Midnight. The map told him he was a few

hundred metres from Sandy Shore Beach. 'Up periscope,' he said to himself and pressed a button.

The hulk of the sub remained under the surface but Jimmy put his eye to the periscope, switching on the night-vision.

It was perfect. With all the patrols in force, hardly anyone was keeping an eye on the beach itself.

Jimmy watched as a policeman who was guarding Sandy Shore Beach in the darkness headed towards the toilet block. The coast was clear. Jimmy eased the submarine forward into the shallow water, being careful not to ground his machine. When he thought he was close enough to the beach, the submarine surfaced, its eyes and teeth gleaming in the moonlight.

'Time to get dirty,' he cackled, pulling on a lever to release the huge jet-sprays that fired oil across the beach. It was all over in less than a minute. The sub sank beneath the surface and reversed out of the bay.

Jimmy set the coordinates for Pleasure Island. He looked in the mirror and saluted at the reflection of the infamous Toxic Terror. 'Just one more beach to go!'

It wasn't until daylight when the townsfolk awoke that the true horror was revealed. Blue Bay and Pleasure Island were now the only clean Blue Flag beaches in Britain.

11. A Million-to-One Chance

Mr Big wasn't one to wait around. He had done his homework on nuclear waste and come up with a plan. He followed the lorry, keeping a discreet distance. He was reassured by the skull and crossbones sign on the back of the wagon, and the words 'toxic' and 'hazardous'. He'd trailed the lorry since it had left the nuclear power plant and he knew that the driver would have to take a break sooner rather than later.

Sure enough, the lorry and its nuclear cargo pulled into a motorway service station and Mr Big pulled up a short distance away. He watched as the driver emerged from the cab, stretched, and wandered in for his motorway service-station lunch. Mr Big pressed a direct-dial button on his mobile phone.

'Yes?' answered Jimmy.

'We're all systems go,' said Mr Big, swinging his metal leg from the lorry cab.

Mr Big wasn't going to carry out this part of the plan. He knew his face didn't fit. The eye-patch, the dodgy leg. 'Give you a parrot and you'd look like Long John Silver!' Jimmy had remarked. So Mr Big had hired a beautiful young lady instead, who had been following in the car behind. As he limped into the service station, his foot clanking on the tiled floor, he saw her get out of her car and walk over to the restaurant.

From outside, Mr Big watched as the truck driver filled his tray and took a seat in the restaurant. The criminal sidekick gave the thumbs-up to the lady and in she went to carry out their plan. She walked up to the lorry driver with a huge grin on her face as she threw a handful of confetti into the air and exploded a party popper over his lunch. 'Congratulations, sir!' she beamed. 'May I see your receipt?'

The lorry driver looked down at the confetti in his soup and then up at the gorgeous lady. He smiled back, and handed her the receipt.

'I thought so,' she shrieked, clapping her hands enthusiastically. 'You, sir, are the one

millionth customer to have bought, er, lasagne and chips,' she said, looking down at his meal. 'The one millionth in this very restaurant!' she squealed.

The man looked confused. 'I am . . .?'

'You most certainly are, sir,' she beamed. All the other customers had gone quiet and were looking their way. 'And we can't let our one millionth customer go unrewarded.'

'You can't . . .?'

'No, we most certainly cannot, sir,' she gushed. 'So you are the proud winner of five hundred pounds' worth of goodies. But you can only claim your prize at *this* service station and within the next *thirty* minutes. So you have to spend, spend, spend!'

'Spend, spend, spend . . .?'

'Now, now, *now*,' encouraged the lady. 'Anything you want. To the value of five hundred pounds!'

'Wow,' nodded the man, forgetting his confetti soup.

'Plus,' smiled the lady. 'You get a free tank of diesel for your lorry. Give me your keys and I'll arrange for it to be filled up while you spend, spend, spend!'

'Fill, fill, fill,' he replied, jumping from his seat. He rummaged for his lorry keys and handed them to the lady. 'See you in thirty minutes,' he declared, as he sprinted off to the shops.

The lady placed the lorry keys into her handbag and beamed at the other customers. One man was looking sadly at his lasagne and chips. 'Sorry, no prizes for a million and one,' she sang as she flounced out of the restaurant, slipping the keys to the pirate look-alike standing by the door as she went.

Mr Big clanked out behind her, crossing the

forecourt as quickly as he could, and hauled himself into the toxic lorry. He put the driver's stolen keys into the ignition and sparked the engine into life. Then he manoeuvred the wagon into the next car park, out of sight of the service station, before swapping cabs. His own lorry had been specially chosen to be the same make and model as the nuclear wagon. Mr Big checked the inside of the cab to make sure he'd not left any clues. Then he checked the number plates. 'The same,' he grinned. 'Identical lorries in every respect.' Mr Big drove the impostor lorry to exactly the same spot as the original and parked it up before returning the keys to his accomplice, along

with an envelope filled with cash. 'Done,' he said.

Back inside, the lady found the man queuing at the checkout with fifty bags of wine gums, thirty CDs and a cuddly toy. 'For my daughter,' he smiled weakly.

She made sure his goodies were paid for so he didn't suspect anything until it was too late, and even helped him load them into his cab.

In the car park nearby, Mr Big had pulled a huge tarpaulin over the barrel shape of the toxic lorry. The deadly cargo was now disguised as 'Jimmy's Donuts'. Delighted with how perfectly his plan had gone, Mr Big pulled the nuclear wagon on to the motorway and headed straight for Pleasure Island.

12. Mission Control

'It's amazing,' sang Ollie. 'Pleasure Island Resort is even *better* than the adverts on telly!'

'And what great weather,' said Ben, tying his jumper around his waist. 'Look, there's a firework display tonight,' he said, pointing at a billboard.

'Check out the beach,' said Sophie, running towards the shoreline.

The children took off their shoes and ran across the warm golden sand, whooping with delight. Ben threw a Frisbee for the puppies, Star leaping to catch it in her mouth. Lara was already up to her chest in the cool ocean, watching as Spud snapped and yapped at the waves. The children rolled up their trousers and paddled up to their knees. A big wave caught Ollie and he squealed as his jeans went dark blue.

Lara looked around at the crowded beach. She knew from what Mr and Mrs Cook had said that Pleasure Island Resort was booked solid for the whole summer. 'We're lucky to be here,' she woofed to the puppies. Lara couldn't help feeling sorry for all the victims of the Toxic Terror. She had her paws crossed that the evil villain wouldn't strike at Pleasure Island.

The children wandered back to the apartment, chatting excitedly as they went. Ben rang the bell and Mum opened the door to everyone bursting in, eager to tell their parents about the beach, sea, funfair and fireworks. Dad was watching the news, tutting about a report from Sandy Shore and a breaking news story about the theft of a lorry from a nuclear power plant.

Just then Spud spied a lorry driving through the gates. 'Jimmy's Donuts,' he woofed. He looked at the sun and estimated the time. *Way past afternoon-tea time*, he thought. *And we're probably not eating until late. And Dad said we couldn't afford big meals. So maybe I could sneak a snack now to quieten my tummy.* He was slobbering. Spud licked his lips and doggy drool sprayed everywhere. *And donuts are in my top five*, he thought. *Along with custard creams . . . Jammie Dodgers . . .*

Mum's cottage pie . . . stew and dumplings . . . candy floss . . . Well, maybe there's more than five! His mind was made up. 'See you guys in a bit,' he woofed. 'I'm off to explore a bit more.'

'Be careful,' woofed Lara. 'Don't wander too far from the apartment.'

Spud nodded and trotted away, his tail

sticking out like an aerial, his nose to the floor. His one-track mind was tuned in to donuts!

He followed the lorry up a small hill on the island and watched as it reversed into the garage of a house with a big *PRIVATE PROPERTY* sign outside. He waited for the unloading of the donuts. *I hope they accidentally drop one – or a box – or a crate . . . enough to fill a young pup's tum.* Nothing seemed to be happening and then the garage doors came down. Spud decided to investigate. He jumped on to a crate and peered in through an open window. Inside, the lorry looked like it was slowly descending on a giant lift.

No way, he thought, squeezing through the tight gap of the window. *The donuts are getting away!* Spud jumped to the ground and quickly scurried underneath the lorry as the lift gently lowered. He crouched in the darkness until all the beeping had stopped, then listened as the lorry door creaked open and a metal foot scraped on the ground.

Yikes! he thought, *what's that? The Terminator?* He watched as the man limped across to another man who was waiting in the strange underground room. *What's going on?* thought Spud. *Where are the donuts?* The puppy sniffed hard, his sensitive doggy nose taking in the smells of the cave. *I can smell the ocean*, he thought. *And a horrible thing*. His nostrils flared and he stopped sniffing because it hurt his nose. Spud's eyes were watering and he had to stop himself choking. *Poison!* he thought. *That's not donuts, it's something dangerous!*

Spud crept out from underneath the lorry and surveyed the scene. Even though he'd failed the assault course he couldn't help going into Spy Pup alert mode. His hackles raised and his brain sprang into action. *One cave. Two men. One lorry*, he observed. *And one submarine? This is very strange indeed*. Spud scampered across to an oil drum and hid from the men. He pricked his doggy ears and tuned in to their conversation.

'Nuclear waste, as agreed,' said the man with the robotic leg, who also wore an eye-patch. 'Grade A. One hundred per cent deadly.'

'Excellent,' purred the other man, who was very old and wrinkled. 'Let's get loaded. We sail tonight. By tomorrow, we'll have raised the pollution bar. The one remaining beach will be wiped out – forever – and bookings at Pleasure Island will reach an all-time high.'

Spud gulped. *Oh dear*, he thought. *The Toxic Terror is right here, on this island. Official Spy Pup or not, I think I might have stumbled across my first proper mission!*

13. The Great Escape

Spud waited for the right moment. *I have to get help*, he thought. *I can't tackle these men on my own. Ma will know what to do, but how do I get out of here?*

The man with the metal leg and eye-patch strolled back to the lorry. There was something familiar about him but Spud couldn't work out what. *I definitely haven't met anyone who looks like that before. Maybe all bad guys look the same!* The man spent a few minutes struggling to get into a special suit. *Wow*, gasped Spud. *He looks like a spaceman!*

Mr Big secured his helmet in place and switched on his oxygen pack. He was taking no chances. He was about to transfer highly toxic nuclear waste from the lorry to the submarine. Beside him, Jimmy struggled into his protective gear too.

Spud knew he had to escape. *Not only from the baddies*, he panicked. *But from the deadly poison that's about to be released. But how?* The spaceman was fiddling with the back of the lorry, his thick gloves making it difficult to open the door. Spud took his chance. There was only one way out. He scampered across the cave floor, his claws tapping rather too loudly. *There's a small inflatable dinghy close to the water's edge. Maybe I can make my way out to sea and sail back to the beach?* Spud knew his plan wasn't guaranteed to work, but he figured that staying put could mean a slow and poisonous death. And he needed to warn everyone about the Toxic Terror.

He ran as fast as his stubby legs would take him. Spud remembered his near-death experience with the lieutenant but knew he had no choice. *Another watery adventure!* He leapt off the rocky jetty towards the dinghy, landing half-in and half-out.

Mr Big and Jimmy looked up. 'What was that?' came the muffled voice of Mr Big. The criminals walked, in slow motion, like men on the moon, to the water's edge. Mr Big was horrified to see a small black puppy scrambling up the side of the dinghy.

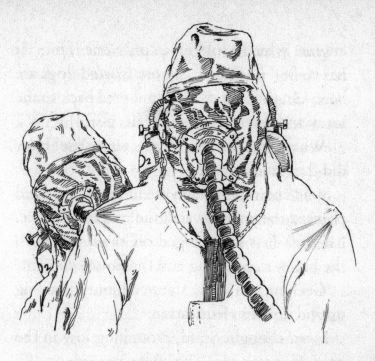

Mr Big's mind was racing. He couldn't be sure but he thought he recognized the dog. *It can't be*, he said to himself.

The puppy's back legs kicked wildly before he eventually hauled himself into the boat. He shook himself down and raced over to fiddle with the outboard motor. *Fuel switched on*, thought Spud. *Check. Choke on. Check*. He tugged at the starter cord with all his energy and the engine spluttered into life.

Mr Big couldn't believe what he was seeing. It wasn't every day you saw a dog start an engine, which could mean only one thing. 'It has to be!' he yelled. 'Those blasted dogs are here. On this island!' He lumbered back to the lorry and reached inside for his pistol.

'What?' said Jimmy. 'That's impossible! How did they find us here?'

Spud chewed through the mooring rope and pointed the boat towards the exit to the cave. Mr Big's first shot pinged off the rocky wall, the bullet ricocheting and the noise echoing.

'Get him, you idiot!' shouted Jimmy, jumping up and down in frustration.

Yikes! thought Spud, crouching low in the boat. *He's got a gun!* The boat chugged steadily towards his escape route. Luckily for the puppy, Mr Big's thick gloves made it difficult to aim. The next bullet hit the boat with a thud, air hissing from the hole. It only took a few seconds for one side of the boat to deflate and water started spilling in. Spud's head was bowed and he couldn't see where he was going. *I just hope I'm heading out of this cavern*, he thought. *Away from those dangerous men*.

The boat struck the cave wall and Spud was nearly thrown overboard. He righted himself but the boat was taking on a lot of water. He glanced at the men in their protective suits. The gun was raised again, pointing his way. Two more bullets zapped into the water and Spud raced away towards the exit. Safely behind the rock, he zig-zagged the boat through the twisty tunnel.

'I'm out!' he barked, as the boat spluttered out of the side of the cliff face. He squinted in the daylight. *But the boat's not very shipshape.* Spud used his paws to scoop water over the side but it was coming in much faster than the small puppy could bail out. He managed to round the headland but the dinghy was sinking. He could see the beach just a few hundred metres away when, eventually, the boat stopped moving altogether.

Spud leapt into the ocean and his legs worked like pistons as he propelled himself through the sea.

Spud's paws finally touched the sand. A wave crashed over him, sending him sprawling on to the beach. The puppy lay for a minute, sopping and exhausted. *No time for a proper rest*, he thought. *I have an adventure to solve. A nuclear attack to stop. This has to be a real mission, surely!* The puppy staggered along the sandy beach towards the Cooks' apartment. *I can't wait to tell Ma!*

Quick to recover his strength, Spud raced along the row of apartments, and scratched at the door of his holiday home. Nobody answered. He howled like a wolf. 'Come on, guys,' he barked. 'This is an emergency. Nuclear attack! Let me in!'

A tourist was walking past who took pity on the howling puppy and rang the doorbell. Mum answered the door and thanked the man as Spud scampered in. He stood in the middle of the lounge and shook himself, water and sand spraying the apartment walls. 'Spud,' began Lara, 'look at the mess you've made.'

'Not as much mess as there's going to be tonight, Ma,' woofed the puppy. Spud barked out what he'd seen while Lara and Star listened intently. It was hard to believe, so Lara asked Spud to tell the story again, but more slowly. 'A robot in a spacesuit?' she said. 'An underground bunker? And a submarine . . . loaded with nuclear waste? Are you sure you haven't just eaten too much candyfloss or fallen asleep in the sunshine, son?'

'It's all true, Ma,' woofed Spud. 'Bullets and

everything! And, the worst thing of all,' he
panted, collapsing to the floor with exhaustion,
'. . . no donuts!'

14. Followed

Lara, Spud and Star locked themselves in the bedroom. 'We need to think this through,' Lara woofed. 'I don't want to frighten the family. But we have to check this out.'

'Have I done well, Ma? Is it a proper mission, Ma?' wagged Spud. 'My first one? Is it? Please say it is.'

Lara sighed. 'If it is, Spud,' she warned, 'it's going to be very dangerous. If the Toxic Terror is here, on this island, it's crucial that we capture him and save the planet from any more harm. Especially if things are going to get as serious as you think.'

'So what do we do next, Mum?' wagged Star.

Lara glanced at Spud. 'We have to check out his story first,' she said. 'It's not that I don't believe you, but if we're going to get the police involved, we need to be sure of the facts.'

'Of course, Ma,' he nodded. 'That's in the top ten rules for Spy Dogs!'

'So,' she asked, 'can you remember where this submarine is?'

Spud's tail was straighter than ever and his nose twitched. 'You bet!' he woofed. 'Just follow me.'

Lara opened the wardrobe and found the professor's backpack, full of gadgets. She struggled into it. 'Are you both wearing the professor's tracking devices?' she asked.

'Always!' replied the two pups, turning to show her their collars.

'OK, then let's go. Stay quiet.' Lara nosed the door open and she and the puppies sneaked out. 'We have to get out before the kids see us,' she barked softly. 'Otherwise they'll tag along, and we can't allow the children to get into trouble.'

Star nodded. She knew what her mum meant. Mrs Cook would go ballistic if the children had any more adventures. When Lara stopped at the apartment door, Star knew what to do. She jumped on to her mum's back, then on to her head and reached for the door handle. Just as the latch clicked, Ollie came out of the bathroom.

'Hi, dogs,' he waved. 'Where are you off to?'

Oh, nowhere in particular, shrugged Lara. *Just popping out for a walkies. That kind of thing.* The three dogs tried to look casual.

'And why have you got your backpack on, Lara?' Ollie quizzed. 'That's the one the professor gave you. Gadgets. For emergencies only,' he frowned.

Yes, well, this is an emergency, thought Lara, nosing at the door and allowing the pups to squeeze through.

Our secret, waved Spud as the apartment door shut behind him.

Ollie wandered into the lounge where Ben and Sophie were watching TV. He plonked himself on the sofa between them. 'The dogs have gone out,' he said, matter-of-factly. 'With the gadget rucksack.'

Ben looked at his little brother. 'Say that again . . .'

'Dogs have gone out,' he smiled. 'With the gadget —'

He didn't need to finish his sentence before

Ben and Sophie were out of their seats and running for the door. If there was an adventure to be had, they wanted to be part of it!

'Hey, wait for me!' shouted Ollie, racing after them.

As soon as they got outside, Sophie spied Spud's wet paw prints. The three children sprinted as fast as Ollie's legs would go. They ran past the arcade and ski dome. Ben saw Spud's tail disappear round a corner.

'There!' he shouted. 'Thankfully Spud's lagging behind as always.' The children raced up a hill and arrived at a garage just as Spud disappeared through the window.

'Look,' said Sophie, pointing to the *PRIVATE PROPERTY* sign.

Ben walked past it and headed for the window. 'We know what *that* means,' he said.

'Yes, that someone's hiding something!' said Sophie, following him. 'C'mon, Ollie.'

'They're up to something,' Ben said. 'Come on, guys, let's follow.'

Sophie was first through the window. It was a tight squeeze but her gymnastics meant she was very flexible. Ollie needed a leg up from his brother and was through. Ben pulled up an oil drum and climbed on top of it. He got stuck halfway and Sophie had to pull hard from inside the garage. Eventually, after a lot of grazing on his sides and tummy, Ben was also through. The children stood in the garage and

looked around. It was empty. 'The dogs came in,' he said. 'We saw them.'

'But they're not here,' noted Sophie, sticking out her bottom lip in puzzlement.

'It's a mystery,' said Ollie. 'The Case of the Disappearing Dogs,' he said in a dramatic-sounding voice.

The children snooped around but there didn't seem to be any other way in or out. 'It *is* a complete mystery,' said Ben, leaning against a vice. All of a sudden there was a whirring noise and the garage floor began to move.

'What's going on?' said Sophie. 'The floor is dropping!'

The children froze on the spot, eyes darting around, as they descended into the ground.

15. Sinking Feeling

As the children came down into the cave they gasped in amazement. 'It's huge!' whispered Ben. They could see Jimmy's living quarters carved into the rock. There was a lorry parked nearby, its diesel engine ticking over. Ben noticed lots of hazard signs on the side of the truck. There was a rocky ledge and, most amazing of all, a huge black submarine was visible in the channel.

Ollie jabbed a finger towards the sub. 'It's got eyes,' he hissed, widening his for effect. 'And teeth!'

'And there's two Martians,' gasped Ben, pointing to two men in radiation suits. Jimmy and Mr Big had been too busy working out what to do about the escaped puppy and their evil plan to notice the lift coming down twice.

Sophie nodded towards Lara and the puppies, who were hiding behind an oil drum. The children watched as the two men fiddled with something in the lorry. They emerged, carrying a small rocket. 'It's a missile,' gasped Ben. 'And by the looks of what they're wearing, a nuclear one!'

'What's "nuclear"?' asked Ollie as the lift reached the cave floor. It made a small clunk as it touched the ground but thankfully Jimmy and Mr Big were now inside the submarine, loading the missile into place.

'It's like a normal rocket but a billion times worse,' hissed Sophie. 'It's the most toxic thing ever!'

'What's "toxic"?' asked Ollie.

'Poison,' whispered Ben as they all tiptoed over to join the dogs. 'Now keep quiet.'

'So *nuclear* toxic is really bad?'

Ben turned and glared at his little brother. No words were needed.

Star and Spud nearly jumped out of their skins as the children approached. Lara smacked a paw against her forehead in frustration.

No way, she thought. *How am I going to explain this to Mrs Cook? 'Erm, sorry but I've accidentally got your kids involved in a missile plot. And there's a submarine! Oh, and it's nuclear.'* But there wasn't time to worry as she beckoned the children to crouch low.

They all watched and waited as the missile was loaded on to the submarine. Then the hatch opened and the men climbed out. They walked towards the office area, right past the dogs, undoing their orange uniforms as they went. Jimmy removed his helmet and Lara's eyes grew wide in amazement.

Jimmy! she thought. *The mad inventor. I've encountered him before! 100% evil.*

Mr Big undid his helmet and Sophie stifled a small cry. She looked at Lara and jabbed a finger towards the man. 'Mr Big,' she mouthed. 'The most horriblest baddie on the planet. With a metal leg and a pirate eye-patch. I thought he was dead.'

We hoped *he was dead,* agreed Lara. *It seems like everything Spud told me is true. All we need is a plan! Think, Lara, think. Jimmy and Mr Big. This is double trouble! This needs a Spy Dog solution.*

The men retreated into the office. 'Star,' Lara woofed quietly, 'you're the smallest and quickest. Follow me and let's see if we can find

out what's going on. Those men are Jimmy and Mr Big, two of the evilest baddies on the planet, so be careful!'

Mr Big? thought Spud. *I thought I recognized him. Yikes, that's bad news!*

Star and her mum crept forward, skulking like prairie wolves, tummies and tails low, hackles raised. They stood outside the door and listened.

Inside the office, the men were finalizing their plan. 'So we're good to go,' said Jimmy. 'I'll captain the sub. You stay here at HQ.'

Mr Big nodded his head. 'It'll take you less than an hour to get there. Then you release the missile and the last remaining beach is sorted.'

'Nuked!' giggled Jimmy. 'So, sorted for good.'

'And Pleasure Island Resort will be the number-one holiday destination!'

'It'll be the *only* holiday destination with a Blue Flag beach,' laughed Jimmy. 'I love it when a plan comes together.' He looked up at the bank of TV monitors in his office. Jimmy liked detail. He had every centimetre of the island covered . . . including his cave. He nudged Mr Big and pointed to one of the screens, his other hand with a finger on his lips.

'What?'

'That,' he mouthed, pointing to the CCTV monitor that showed pictures of the cave. 'Intruders!'

Before Star knew what was happening, Jimmy had flung the door open and grabbed her by the collar. Lara jumped at the man and sank her teeth into his ankle. Jimmy screamed, dropped Star and kicked hard. Lara fell backwards and Jimmy bent down quickly to pick Star up again before she had a chance to get away. The puppy wriggled and growled for all her worth but couldn't free herself from his grip. 'Stay, big dog,' he warned, 'or the little dog gets it.'

16. Sub Pup

Lara snarled. She circled the man, baring her sharp teeth. Mr Big appeared with a baseball bat, slapping it menacingly into his hand.

'We meet again,' he smiled.

Jimmy held the wriggling puppy at arm's length. 'You know this dog?' he asked.

'We've met several times,' growled Mr Big. 'Mummy dog,' he said, pointing to Lara, 'they call her Spy Dog. GM something or other. And that puppy is responsible for this,' he said, pointing to his eye-patch. 'And this,' he added, pointing to his bionic leg.

'We seem to have a lot in common,' agreed Jimmy, 'because big dog here,' he waved Star in Lara's direction, 'put an end to my ozone mission. She's already saved the planet once. But she's not going to save it again.' He looked back at the bank of TV screens. 'Kids,' he bellowed. 'Come out, come out, wherever you are.'

Ben, Sophie and Ollie stood up from behind the oil drum, hands raised like they'd seen people do in the movies. 'We surrender,' shouted Ben. 'Please don't hurt our puppy.'

Jimmy narrowed his eyes at the children. 'If

you want your puppy to grow into an adult dog, you'd better do what I say. OK?'

'OK,' chorused the children. Ben was trembling with anger, Sophie with fear.

Ollie frowned at Jimmy. 'I don't like baddies,' he said.

'And I don't like children,' Jimmy spat.

'Or dogs,' added Mr Big. 'There's a saying,' he snarled, '"never work with children or animals".'

Behind the oil drum Spud stayed safely out of view. *He hasn't spotted me yet. But I still need a plan to stop this disaster!*

Star wriggled for her life. She kicked out at the man – *Let me go, you horrible baddie* – but she was tiny and his grip was strong. 'Don't worry about me, Ma,' she woofed. 'He's the Toxic Terror. Attack him before he launches that deadly missile.'

Lara's mind whirred. This was what the professor called a 'code A red', the worst possible scenario. Her priority was the safety of the young ones. *The Cooks' and my own!* She noticed that Spud was nowhere to be seen. *Hiding*, she thought. *That's my boy.*

Jimmy ushered Lara and the children into

the office and shut the door. He plonked Star on to the table with a thud, sending her snout into the wood. Her nose started bleeding and her eyes watering. Lara growled her loudest growl but Jimmy kept a firm grip. He knew that if he let go, his bargaining power was gone and the Spy Dog would attack.

'Amendment to the plan,' Jimmy said to Mr Big. 'You stay here with the brats and dogs,' he suggested, 'while I take the submarine and finish our plans. When I get back we can decide what to do.'

Mr Big grinned. 'I know what to do already,' he beamed, his gold teeth glinting. 'I used to have dreams about Spy Dog in prison,' he snarled. 'Except they were dreams about a *dead dog*.'

Star wriggled again and received another pounding on the table top. Jimmy handed the puppy to Mr Big. His grip on her collar was even tighter.

Lara felt helpless. She glanced at the CCTV pictures and saw Spud scurrying towards the submarine. *Be careful, son – don't get caught.* She watched from the corner of her eye as the puppy jumped on to the metal monster and disappeared down the hatch. She knew what

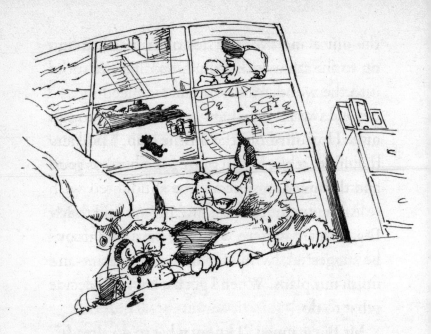

Spud was doing was highly dangerous, but she couldn't see any other way he could stop Jimmy and Mr Big from carrying out their evil plan. Once the submarine left the cave, there was no turning back. *Go, Spud*, she thought. *You are our only chance. It's your big moment to save the world.*

Jimmy marched across the rocky floor towards the submarine and jumped on to the top of it. The small gathering watched from the office window as Jimmy waved, before disappearing into the hatch.

It was a very big submarine. Jimmy had

bought it a few years ago from a foreign government, no questions asked. The hatch lid closed and he prepared to set sail.

Spud was glad there were plenty of places to hide. He sniffed out the missile launch pod and hid under a blanket in one of the bunks. Spud heard the hatch shut and he shuddered with fear. He knew he wasn't a fully qualified Spy Dog but he was about to go on a dangerous voyage in a tin can under the sea. He wasn't sure he could stop the missile but he was certainly going to give it his best shot.

17. Leg Irons

Mr Big had tied one of Lara's front legs to the table. He'd put Star in a filing cabinet and shut the drawer. Ben, Sophie and Ollie could hear the Spy Pup's muffled yapping as they sat quietly, their faces pale and drawn. 'You'll never get away with it,' said Ben bravely.

'Looks like we already have,' corrected Mr Big. 'Like all plans, it's *deadly* simple.' Mr Big laughed so hard it triggered his smoker's cough. The children grimaced. Even his cough was criminal. They watched and waited as he swilled some phlegm around his mouth. He looked uncomfortable – what he'd coughed up was obviously too horrible to swallow. '*Deadly* simple,' he grinned, spitting a black blob into the sink. 'One last trip in the submarine. Jimmy's loaded what we call a "dirty bomb".

It won't create a big mushroom cloud. But it will kill all life on the Blue Bay coastline for many years to come.'

'I don't like mushrooms,' said Ollie, matter-of-factly. 'Or broccoli either.'

Mr Big's eyebrows slanted downwards in puzzlement. Children had always been a mystery. He went to the fridge and opened the door. 'I need a beer,' he said, cradling a cold bottle. 'Where's that bottle-opener?' he grumbled, rummaging in the cutlery drawer.

Lara woofed at Ben. Then she whined. *My backpack*, she thought. *Get him to look in there*.

Ben looked puzzled. 'What?' he mouthed to his dog.

Gadgets! Lara jabbed towards the bag with her only free paw.

Ben's brain clicked into gear. 'I think Lara has a bottle-opener in her backpack,' he suggested. 'She always carries one, you know, in case of emergencies.'

Mr Big looked unsure. *A dog with a backpack*, he thought. *Most unusual*. 'No funny stuff, mutt, or the kids get it, OK?'

Lara nodded as he approached. She couldn't help but curl her lip. *I absolutely hate baddies. The more evil they are, the more I dislike them! And they don't come more evil than Bionic Big!*

Mr Big unclipped the backpack and peered inside. He tipped it up and poured the contents on to the table. There were gadgets galore. 'No opener,' he growled, rummaging through the items.

Ben saw the Mega Magnet. Lara caught his eye. *Are you thinking what I'm thinking?* she thought. *Metal leg? Powerful magnet?*

Ben winked at his dog. 'She's a Spy Dog,' explained Ben, 'so she has gadgets. Like James Bond except she's real and he's imaginary. Gadgets like this one,' said Ben, pointing. 'It's a torch that shines in the daytime.'

Mr Big dissolved into peals of laughter, just long enough for Sophie to grab the Mega Magnet and throw it to Ollie. Ollie closed his hand around it. He smiled at Mr Big. He was only six but he understood. 'I need a wee,' he said, getting up from his seat and wandering towards the door.

'Oh no you don't, sonny Jim,' said Mr Big, catching the boy by his arm. 'You stay put.' He swung Ollie back into his seat.

But it was too late. Ollie's job was done – the

gadget was attached to Mr Big's metal leg. Now someone just needed to press the red button and the world's most powerful magnet would be activated.

'I need one too,' said Sophie, standing up. Mr Big pushed her back into her seat but she just had time to reach out towards the magnet. The children and Lara threw themselves to the floor as Sophie pressed the button.

As soon as the magnet was activated, cutlery

hurled itself at Mr Big. Knives pinged across the room, sticking themselves to his robotic leg. One of the metal forks missed his leg and embedded itself in the villain's bottom. There was a blood-curdling scream as his other buttock was punctured by a corkscrew. The metal filing cabinets closed in around him and the evil baddie disappeared under half a ton of metal objects from around the office. All the children could see was a bionic foot poking out of the mess. Mr Big's whimpering sounded pitiful.

Ben opened the filing-cabinet drawer and out popped Star. Lara was released and Ben went straight to the phone. He dialled Professor Cortex's mobile number. 'It's an emergency, Professor,' he explained. 'I think you need to come quickly.'

18. Bat Man

Spud peeped out from under the blanket. The submarine had been going for nearly an hour and Jimmy had loaded the nuclear missile into the launch pod, ready to fire.

Jimmy picked up the radio mic. 'Jimmy calling the Big man,' he began. 'Are you receiving? Over.'

Spud was relieved to hear Ben answer. 'Over's the right word, you horrible crook. Your *dastardly plot* is over,' he said bravely. 'We've captured Big and you're next.'

Jimmy failed to hide his surprise. 'Children and animals, eh? You've overpowered Metallic Man. Useless hunk of metal!' He glanced at the radar. 'Never mind. I'm in range of the beach,' he said calmly. 'Good effort, kiddie-winks,' he admitted, 'but a bit too late to stop me. In less than five minutes my plan will be activated. Over and out!' He smiled an evil wrinkly grin as the submarine powered towards its final destination.

Spud listened intently. He knew he needed to do something but wasn't sure what. He peeped from under the blanket again. Jimmy was looking at a radar screen.

'Nearly there,' he heard him say. 'Let the fireworks begin.'

OK, thought Spud, *it's now or never. If he wants action, I'd better give him some.* The puppy nuzzled himself out from under the blanket. A chill went up his spine as he crept forward.

Jimmy was pouring himself a glass of champagne. 'May as well savour the moment of destruction,' he said to himself as the bubbles fizzed up and over the top of the glass.

By now Spud was behind him. He could see the big red button marked LAUNCH. *Right, three . . . two . . . one . . .*

Jimmy knocked back the champagne and gave a loud belch. 'A toast,' he shouted to himself, 'to genius, planning and eternal wealth.'

Just as Jimmy's hand reached for the button, Spud launched himself. He hurled his chubby body at Jimmy's arm and sank his razor-sharp teeth into the man's wrist. Jimmy yelled and champagne spilled everywhere. Spud could feel himself being swung around but he held on, his teeth sinking deeper. Jimmy swung the puppy against the metal wall and Spud had to let go. He fell to the floor with a thump.

Down but not out. He attacked again. *The world depends on me*, he thought as he darted for the man's ankle. Spud received a kick for his troubles, sending him shooting into the air. He landed on the submarine's huge control panel, dazed.

Jimmy's ankle and hand were bleeding badly as he reached down beside the captain's seat to grab something. 'Come here, you pesky little mutt.'

He sure looks angry, thought Spud as the man staggered towards him, a metal baseball bat raised. Spud rolled away as the first hit sent sparks flying across the control panel. The next wallop was too close for comfort.

Slam! Down came the third strike, but this one caught the puppy and he yelped and limped away. Now Spud was cornered. His leg felt numb. Jimmy's nostrils were flaring as he raised the bat one more time. Spud put his front paws up to his face to protect himself but then leapt aside at the final second as the bat came down with an almighty crash. The control panel's computer screen shattered. The electrics fizzed and the submarine was plunged into darkness.

After a few seconds the emergency lighting kicked in and an orangey glow lit the submarine. All was silent except for the beep of the sonar. The power cut had been just long enough for Spud to sniff out his escape in the darkness. He cowered back under the blanket, hidden from sight.

Jimmy cursed and lowered his bat. 'OK, puppy,' he admitted, breathing like a bull. 'You win.'

'What's happening down there?' Professor

Cortex's voice yelled out over the radio. He'd followed Star's tracking device, dragging Mr and Mrs Cook down into the cave. Mrs Cook had almost fainted at the sight of the radiation warning sign on the side of the lorry.

The small crowd strained their ears, listening for a reply. 'Agent Spud,' the professor tried again. 'Are you OK? Over.' He held the microphone out towards Lara.

'Spud,' she yapped. 'Don't do anything to put your life at risk! The police are on their way. Over.'

Spud wanted to reply but kept himself hidden. *It was a bit hairy*, he thought. *It was nearly all over. Over!*

'Has the missile been launched, Agent Spud? Over,' asked the professor, trying to sound calm.

Jimmy grabbed at the radio control and switched it on. 'I don't know who this is,' he bellowed, 'but it *will* be any moment now. Just time for me to escape. Over – *once and for all!*' He tapped some buttons on the control panel. Then he pulled an oxygen mask over his face and strapped the tank on to his back. With a tug he pulled open an escape hatch on the floor and let water flood into the submarine.

'Wherever you're hiding, I'm out of here, doggy. And the missile fires in two minutes' time,' he announced, his voice muffled from behind the mask. 'Oh no,' he giggled. 'Silly me . . . one minute and forty-six seconds.' Jimmy jumped towards the hatch and disappeared into the ocean.

Spud had crept out from under the blanket as the water rose, almost over his head now. He glanced at the digital clock as his paws lifted off the floor and he had to start paddling.

Water kept gushing in and Spud had no chance of closing the hatch. 'I need hands not paws,' he barked in frustration. He paddled over to the captain's chair and leapt on to the control panel. He clicked on the radio. 'Ma,' he barked, 'I'm in big trouble!'

19. A Real Mission

Lara's bark came over the radio. 'Hang in there, son,' she said. 'The professor's going to give you instructions on how to stop the nuclear missile. You have to do what he says.'

'But there's water, Ma,' woofed Spud. 'It's coming in so fast.'

'You have to do what the professor asks,' barked Lara. 'You're a real Spy Pup now.'

'Is this a mission, Ma?' woofed Spud. 'Is it a real mission?'

The professor's voice came next. 'Agent Spud,' he said, 'we have just over one minute left. If the missile hits the beach it will kill people . . . wildlife . . . the whole eco-system . . . for hundreds of years. I've looked at the layout of the sub and the missile system. Unfortunately, we don't have time to stop the launch. Instead, you need to turn the submarine around. That way, the missile will shoot harmlessly out to sea. It will rest on the ocean floor until we can retrieve it. Bark once if you understand me. Over.'

'Woof,' barked Spud. The water was a third of the way up the side of the sub and gushing in as fast as ever. *Quick, Prof, before the backup generator short-circuits.* Spud listened carefully for the next instruction.

'There's a joystick,' shouted the professor, looking at the submarine plans that Sophie had spread out on the office desk. His voice was barely audible above the rush of water. 'Like on an old video game. Over.'

Spud barked once. *Yes, sir, I can see it. I'm good at video games, Prof.*

'Pull the throttle sharp left for as long as you can, Agent Spud. And we might just have a chance of turning the sub. Over.'

Spud's heart sank. 'But the joystick is nearly underwater,' he yelped. Spud knew he had no choice. He was determined to defeat the Toxic Terror, even if it cost him his life. Spud's stubby legs pumped hard as he swam to the joystick and gripped it between his paws. He pulled it sharp left and the submarine lurched. More water poured in. Spud looked around. *Yikes!* he thought, *the submarine is half full*.

'That's good,' shouted the professor, tracking the sub's moves on the radar screen in Jimmy's cave. 'And again, Agent Spud – the submarine is turning, but it needs to turn faster. We have thirty seconds before launch.'

'Go for it, son,' woofed Lara over the radio. 'You have twenty-five seconds to save the world!'

Spud stretched his neck to keep his face above the surface. His small black nose poked out of the top of the water. He took a deep breath and his nose disappeared. He opened his eyes wide in the darkness, the sea water stinging, his lungs bursting. Spud found the lever again and hung on. He kicked hard and the joystick swung left. Spud kept kicking until his eyes bulged and his air ran out. He exploded back to the surface, gulping down a lungful of oxygen and spluttering in the sea water. There was almost no room to breathe as the water neared the roof. He could no longer hear the radio.

'Ma,' he woofed, even though he knew no

one could hear. 'Is it a mission? Please let it be a real mission.' He choked on a lungful of salty water. 'I think it's my first and last one.'

The submarine shook as the missile launched. Spud's head was now touching the ceiling of the submarine. Soon there would be no air left.

'Yessss!' yelled the professor back in the cave. 'Agent Spud,' he shouted excitedly, 'fine work. The missile is launched but our radar shows it's heading harmlessly out to sea. Over.'

There was no reply.

'Bro,' barked Star, 'can you hear us? You did it!'

Still nothing came from the radio except a crackle. 'Son?' Lara whimpered.

'I'm sure he's fine, GM451,' said the professor, smiling as best he could. 'He's a fighter.' But as Star licked Lara's face and they both curled up on the floor, he looked at Mr and Mrs Cook with a worried expression. Ben, Sophie and Ollie hugged their pets.

'Spud is a hero,' said Ben. 'Just like his mum.'

Back on the submarine, Spud's legs were weary. He'd thought of everything but there were no more options. His oxygen pill had gone – donated to Lieutenant Black. *I've done my very best. Nobody can ask more of me than that.*

The water was so high he could hardly bark. 'I hope I've done well, Ma?' he gurgled, choking on sea water. 'I hope this was a real mission . . .'

20. Dogs United

Jimmy was a decent swimmer. The salt water stung his wrinkles but he didn't mind. His missile was on its way. Blue Bay would be destroyed and his resort would become the number one tourist attraction in the country. He knew he couldn't return, but the profits would still be his. All that lovely cash would be flooding into his offshore bank account.

The water felt icy cold as he made his way slowly upwards towards the light and surfaced. He was a tiny dot in a big ocean. Jimmy took off his mask and turned 360 degrees. He could see a fishing boat in the near distance. Its bright light was sweeping across the ocean to search for buoys that showed where its fishing nets were laid.

'Over here,' Jimmy yelled, waving his arms

in the air as the light swept past him. He smiled with relief as the boat chugged over to pick him up.

'Bit late for a swim, isn't it?' called the fisherman from over the side of the boat. He attached a metal ladder to the side of the boat and Jimmy climbed in.

Jimmy explained that he'd got lost while scuba diving and that he needed dropping off at Pleasure Island. The fisherman believed his lie and was happy to help, especially when Jimmy promised him a hefty payment in return. Jimmy figured that the authorities might be searching for him and that arriving by boat might draw attention. But his car was there and that was his best means of escape if he could somehow get to it. The police probably wouldn't expect him to return to the island after everything that had gone on. He'd decided to take the risk.

When Pleasure Island Beach was in sight, Jimmy thanked the skipper and jumped into the sea. *Here's hoping no one notices an early-morning swimmer*, he thought, heading for the beach.

*

Ben filled his parents in on the finer details. Mum was very angry, but she managed to remain calm. It didn't seem right to shout – not after what had happened to poor Spud.

'And Jimmy and Mr Big wanted to make sure the final part of their plan went with a real bang,' Sophie explained.

'Indeed,' nodded the professor, pushing his spectacles back up to the bridge of his nose. 'They managed to get their hands on some nuclear material, so that final missile would have been a very big bang indeed.'

'Where's the missile now?' asked Ollie.

Professor Cortex checked Jimmy's radar screen for the latest information. He pointed to a flashing light. 'Thanks to our hero puppy,' said the professor, brushing away a tear, 'the missile is resting harmlessly on the seabed, approximately thirty miles off the coast. A Navy vessel is already on its way.'

'And what about Jimmy?' asked Mum. 'Has there been any sighting of that horrible man?'

Professor Cortex shook his head. 'He will have had oxygen,' he said. 'So, provided he made it out of the sub in one piece, he could be anywhere. Maybe a boat picked him up. Or maybe he's swimming for it. Who knows? We've got alerts going out down the coastline to look out for him.' The scientist sank into a chair and sighed deeply. He closed his eyes and shook his head. 'But Spud *didn't* have oxygen and it's all my fault,' he muttered to himself. 'If only I'd given Spud extra pills after he saved Lieutenant Black, I could have saved his life.'

'You didn't know this would happen,' said Mr Cook, trying to make the professor feel better. 'This was supposed to be a holiday, not an adventure!'

Lara lay forlornly, her eyes drooping as much as her shoulders. Her sticky-up ear was at half-mast. *I blame myself*, she thought. *It was me who encouraged Spud to attend spy training. It was me who taught him how to sniff out danger*. Lara's chest heaved with sadness. *My boy*, she howled. *I'm so sorry*.

Star nuzzled closer, the dogs united in grief.

21. Lesser Spotted Jimmy

The Cook family returned to their apartment. The holiday spirit was well and truly extinguished. Sophie was gently weeping. Ben was biting his lip. As always, Ollie seemed fairly upbeat. 'No point moping,' he said. 'Who wants to play on the beach?'

Lara looked at Star. 'Go on, girl,' she encouraged. 'A run on the sand will do you good. And it'll cheer Ollie up too.'

Star didn't feel like having fun but she did what her mum asked. The other two children vegged out in front of the TV while Ollie and Star wandered outside for some fresh air.

They got to the beach and Star looked out to sea, the grey ocean stretching to the horizon. *Poor Spud*, she thought. She kicked a ball about with Ollie for a few minutes, then went in goal while he practised his penalties. Star dived to her left and tipped the ball over the imaginary bar.

'Cool save, Star,' Ollie laughed.

Thanks, she thought, perking up a bit. *It is helping take my mind off things.* Star kicked the ball back to Ollie. She looked at the ocean once more where a few people were splashing around. Most had their trouser legs rolled up and had braved it up to their knees. *Crikey*, she thought, *look at him*. A man emerged from the ocean wearing a face-mask. He looked exhausted, staggering up the beach, his knees wobbling. *An oxygen tank*, noted Star. *But no wetsuit. He's been underwater with no wetsuit! That poor man must be freezing.*

The man waded out of the sea. He looked around the beach and was about to take off his mask when he glanced in Star's direction. Instead he looked quickly away and kept his mask in place, then threw off the tank and hurried nervously up the beach.

Ollie's next penalty hit Star on the back of the head and brought her to her senses. She shook herself alert. Star looked to the shoreline again but the man was gone. *I wonder?* she thought. 'Ollie, you stay there,' she woofed, holding her paw up to signal 'stay'. 'I'm going to check out Mr Face-mask.'

Star bounded across the sand, her little legs a blur of speed. She stood at the end of the beach and looked left, then right. *There he is!* The man was crouched down beside a car. He felt around on top of the front wheel and pulled out a set of keys that were hidden there.

I hope that's his car, she thought. *And he sure looks nervous. He's too far away to identify, especially with that stupid swimming mask on.*

Star bounded towards the man. He opened the car door and pulled a backpack off the front seat. He wriggled into dry clothes and, finally, he peeled off his mask. Star could only see the back of his head. *Hmm . . . I wonder?*

The man turned to check he had escaped. His red eyes met Star's gaze.

Jimmy! she snarled.

'Dratted puppy,' he shouted, jumping into the car, slamming the door and starting the engine.

'You horrible puppy-killer,' yelped Star. 'You'll pay for what you did to my brother!'

The car screeched away, spraying sand in Star's face. She was a super-fit puppy, top of her class, but she was no match for a car. *Think, Star, think. I know!* she remembered. *George's skateboard. Ben brought it on hols. He was going to have a go this morning, he said.*

Star sprinted back to the beach.

'C'mon, Ollie,' she shouted. 'There's a baddie on the loose!'

Ollie raced after Star as she bounded towards the apartment. Ben was just opening the door as they arrived, skateboard under his arm. She jumped up at him, grabbed the skateboard and was out again before he'd realized what was happening.

Ollie watched as Star pulled the ripcord and the skateboard engine spluttered into life. 'That's George's,' he said. 'I don't think it's for dogs.'

Well, this dog is on a mission, she thought. *I can't let Jimmy get away scot-free!* Star had seen George practising on the skateboard. He was always strapped in and then lay flat, using his body weight to steer the professor's invention. *Nought to sixty in five seconds*, she'd heard the professor brag. *I've not got time to strap myself in*, she thought. *So I'll just lie flat and hold on tight.* Star dropped to her tummy. She pressed the accelerator with her nose and she was away. *Puppy versus baddie — it's my turn to be a hero!*

22. The Sixty-Mile-an-Hour Dog

Star went steadily at first, her ears flapping in the wind. The roads were narrow and there were people everywhere. She had a near-miss with an old lady in a wheelchair. 'Oops, sorry,' yapped the speeding dog as she went through the legs of a man walking back from the beach.

Star threw her body right, then left, getting used to steering. Her face was very close to the road. *Yikes*, she thought, *it's whizzing by very fast!* She bumped up a kerb and zoomed on to a straight bit of tarmac. *This is the bridge that connects Pleasure Island to the mainland*, she thought. *Long, straight and very, very fast.* Star pushed her nose against the throttle and the engine screamed. The skateboard shot along at full speed, Star's whiskers and fur blowing in the gale. She hit a drain and was nearly thrown off. *Yikes, that was close!*

As she raced along, she could see Jimmy's get-away car a hundred metres in the distance. He was driving slowly – there was no need to draw attention to himself.

There's a red light up ahead. Oh dear, thought Star, taking a big gulp. *Not sure I can stop in time?*

She was right. The skateboarding dog shot through the lights, engine whining, the canine driver howling. The green man was flashing and pedestrians leapt out of the way as the puppy wailed her way through the junction. She veered under a lorry and heard a squeal of brakes as the driver tried to avoid her. Star shot out the other side. 'Sorry,' she howled. *Can't stop, baddie to catch.*

Jimmy looked in his

rear-view mirror. He could see chaos behind him but couldn't work out what was going on. As he turned on to the motorway, he heard a dog barking

through his left window. He looked out but couldn't see anything. Star had rocketed alongside the moving car. 'Hey, you,' she woofed through the open window, her bark trailing away in the wind. 'Yeah, over here, buddy.'

Jimmy glanced out of the window again. At first he thought he might have swallowed too much salt water and was seeing things. But there, on the hard shoulder of the motorway, was a small dog, lying flat on what seemed to be, of all things, a rocket-powered skateboard. Then he realized. 'Spy Pup,' he cursed.

'Give up!' shouted Star. 'You're under arrest. For killing my brother. And for polluting beaches. For being horrid and for lots of other things too, I expect!'

'You'll never catch me, mutt,' Jimmy yelled. His car was big and Star's skateboard was tiny. It was no contest. He turned the steering wheel towards the skateboard.

Yikes! thought Star, throwing her body weight left to avoid the tyres. The wheels of her board skimmed along the edge of the tarmac and the board started to wobble. She steered back to the right. *I've got to avoid those big black tyres*, she thought, as Jimmy swerved his car left, then right, trying to squash the dog.

By now Jimmy's car was veering all over the motorway. Horns blared as other motorists showed their rage. A police car had seen him and was in pursuit.

'Suspected drunk driver,' radioed the policeman. 'Going north out of Pleasure Island.'

He looked again and shook his head. *Am I seeing things?* 'And . . . er . . . a skateboarding puppy,' he said. 'Request backup.'

Star realized it was too dangerous next to Jimmy's wheels. She hit the throttle once more. The tiny engine screamed and she shot out in front of the car.

'Got you,' he grinned, his foot pressing hard on the accelerator. 'Right where I need you.'

Star couldn't go any faster. She glanced behind as the car came closer. Jimmy looked in his rear-view mirror and saw flashing blue lights. The police siren made him jump and he veered off the road, losing control. His car bounced down a grassy bank and bumped through a field before ending nose-down in a ditch. The bonnet was smashed and the engine was steaming, and Jimmy was pinned in his seat by the air bag.

Star managed to stop the skateboard, gliding to a halt on the hard shoulder. She watched as two more police cars joined the scene and Jimmy was led away. He was yelling something about a skateboarding puppy as the officers sat him in their car and breath-tested him.

'Gotcha!' Star shouted, her tail wagging at top speed. Careful not to be seen by the police, she dragged George's skateboard into a shrub at the side of the motorway.

This one's for you, bro, she thought, wishing Spud was with her to share the excitement like he always had been. With tears running down

her furry face, she trotted towards Pleasure
Island to tell her mum that Jimmy had been
captured.

23. An Unusual Catch

'Haul 'em up,' shouted the skipper. The first mate started winding the winch. It took a very strong man to haul up the catch. His arms bulged, magnifying his mermaid tattoo. The fishing boat bobbed in the water as the net came alongside. Another of the team caught the net with a hook on the end of a pole and pulled it towards the boat. The net was lowered on to the deck and released. Thousands of silvery fish flipped in the daylight. Among the wriggling was a small, dark lifeless shape.

'What's that?' yelled the skipper.

His first mate waded into the wriggling mass and pulled out a small black puppy. He lifted it to show the skipper. 'Dog fish,' he joked. He held the puppy by its neck and shook it. The fish flipped wildly. The black puppy hung

lifeless. He laid the dog out, tummy down, on deck and stroked its back.

'Is it dead?' asked the skipper, coming over to take a closer look.

They both watched as one of the puppy's front paws twitched, and his eyelids fluttered.

'No, I'm not,' choked Spud, opening one eye and coughing up a pint of sea water. 'I'm not a dead dog . . . I'm a Spy Dog.'

Spud's tracking device did the rest. Once it

was dry, it lit up and before they knew it, a Navy vessel had come alongside the fishing boat and Spud had been collected.

Onboard the ship, everyone crowded round to see the puppy that had stopped the Toxic Terror.

'What a hero,' said Commander Green as she stroked Spud's black fur.

'Hey, I recognize that dog!' shouted one man, pushing his way to the front.

Lieutenant Black lifted the puppy up and checked his ear. 'A bullet hole. It must be the same puppy. Looks like you're a Spy Dog after all, pup,' he smiled.

Spud was still feeling weak but he managed to lick the lieutenant's hand as he wrapped him in a blanket.

The puppy was so glad to be alive. After turning the submarine, he'd calculated his odds of survival. *Zero oxygen. It's a one hundred per cent chance of drowning if I stay put*, he'd thought. *And a ninety-nine per cent chance of drowning if I go for it*. The glimmer of hope had been enough for the desperate pup. He'd taken one last lungful of air and escaped from the submarine hatch. His head pounded as he swam upwards as fast as his tiny legs would carry him. Spud remembered seeing the light above but he knew it was too far off. *Darkness below*, he thought. *And light above. I must keep going.* He remembered thinking how small his lungs were and wishing he'd had one of the professor's O24U pills. He'd felt dizzy. His one per cent chance was disappearing. His legs slowed as his air ran out. Then his legs had stopped working altogether, almost as if they'd become tangled together.

Because they had! he thought. *In a fishing net! They say cats have nine lives . . . Well, maybe puppies do too?*

By the time Spud was reunited with his family he was wagging his tail at full-strength, sipping hot chocolate with marshmallows, and re-enacting his Spy Pup adventure for the whole crew.

24. A Special Reward

It was a very special celebration. The residents of Blue Bay had offered the Cooks and their three wonderful dogs a free holiday, and they held a special party to thank them. 'You saved our beach,' explained the mayor. 'And most probably our lives!'

All in a day's work, wagged Star. She was so pleased to have her brother back safe and sound. *And it's a double bonus that I captured Jimmy.*

Spud was delighted that the free holiday also included free food. At one point he began to doubt that he had survived after all. 'Eat and drink as much as you like,' the mayor had smiled.

Am I in heaven? thought the puppy.

'This town owes you so much.' The mayor patted Spud on the head and handed him a whole pizza with extra salami.

Spud wagged harder than he'd ever wagged before. 'Do you think they owe me a lifetime's supply of donuts?' he thought aloud. Lara frowned at him, the look bringing him back to earth.

It was a lovely garden party, followed by games on the beach. The children returned to their holiday home exhausted and flopped down in front of the TV.

'Hey look,' shouted Ben. 'We're on the news.'

The family crowded round the TV. 'That's me,' woofed Spud, jabbing a paw at the TV. 'Eating those sausage rolls.'

'And there's me,' wagged Star, 'with the mayor.'

'And me again,' woofed Spud, 'eating that cheesecake. And those sandwiches. And those biscuits . . .' His woof trailed off as he caught his mum's eye.

'A very special celebration took place in Blue Bay today,' said the reporter. 'As we know, the Cook family – and especially their dogs – saved the town from a nuclear attack. A so-called "dirty bomb" was set for detonation on the Blue Bay coastline. The evil villain behind the plot, Jimmy Tartan, who the country knows as the Toxic Terror, is now behind bars, in the country's maximumest-security prison. His accomplice, Albert Big, has also been locked up after being captured in a way the police described as "most unusual", using cutting-edge science never seen before.'

The children cheered. 'I bet he never wants to see a magnet again!' said Sophie.

Spud danced around, shadow-boxing. *Take that, you baddie*. His attention snapped back to the evening news.

'Tartan and Big were two of Britain's most wanted men,' said the newsreader. A picture of the sullen-faced pair was on screen. The children booed and hissed.

'Good riddance to bad rubbish,' yelled Ollie.

'It seems,' continued the newsreader, 'that Tartan and Big were intent on bringing environmental disaster to beaches across the land, eventually leaving Pleasure Island as the only *clean* destination.'

'But we stopped him,' howled Spud.

'*I* stopped him,' reminded Star, proud of her skateboard chase.

'Shush,' hissed Sophie. 'Stop barking. There's more.'

'Tartan had built up quite an empire. Police describe him as a criminal genius. He'd even created a micro-climate so that Pleasure Island had all-year-round sunshine and good weather, bringing crowds flocking to his resort. Police believe his nightly firework displays were part of the plot. His rockets contained a special cloud-dispersing formula, guaranteeing sunshine, even in the darkest of months.'

Heads nodded around the TV. 'That's genius,' agreed Sophie. 'He really didn't need to be a baddie at all. He could have been a goodie genius.'

'So,' smiled the reporter, 'it seems the plan was *almost* perfect. But a pair of puppies managed to put an end to their hideous crime.'

Star slapped a paw to her head as she saw a picture of herself on TV. *Look at my ears*, she thought. *They're all over the place. Haven't they got a better picture?*

'This adventure involved dangerous criminals, toxic pollution, a submarine and a high-speed skateboard chase.' The newsreader lowered his voice and one of his eyebrows for dramatic effect. 'This was indeed a *real* mission.'

Ben switched off the TV. 'You're both famous!' he said.

'And *both* Spy Dogs,' added Sophie, patting Spud on the head.

Spud sat proudly, his chest puffed out and his neck straight. He wore his new Spy Dog badge with pride. The Secret Service had decided that his adventure had earned him the honour, 'for putting his life in danger in order to protect the country'. He looked at his sister and she wagged hard.

Star cuddled up beside her brother. She knew it was all Spud had ever wanted. *That and unlimited food!*

Bright and shiny and sizzling with fun stuff . . .

puffin.co.uk

WEB FUN

UNIQUE and exclusive digital content!
Podcasts, photos, Q&A, Day in the Life of, interviews
and much more, from Eoin Colfer, Cathy Cassidy,
Allan Ahlberg and Meg Rosoff to Lynley Dodd!

WEB NEWS

The **Puffin Blog** is packed with posts and photos from
Puffin HQ and special guest bloggers. You can also sign up
to our monthly newsletter **Puffin Beak Speak**

WEB CHAT

Discover something new EVERY month –
books, competitions and treats galore

WEBBED FEET

(Puffins have funny little feet and
brightly coloured beaks)

Point your mouse our way today!

It all started with a Scarecrow.

Puffin is seventy years old.
Sounds ancient, doesn't it? But Puffin has never been
so lively. We're always on the lookout for the next big
idea, which is how it began all those years ago.

Penguin Books was a big idea from the mind of
a man called Allen Lane, who in 1935 invented
the quality paperback and changed the world.
**And from great Penguins, great Puffins grew,
changing the face of children's books forever.**

The first four Puffin Picture Books were hatched in 1940 and the
first Puffin story book featured a man with broomstick arms called
Worzel Gummidge. In 1967 Kaye Webb, Puffin Editor, started the
Puffin Club, promising to **'make children into readers'**.
She kept that promise and over 200,000 children became
devoted Puffineers through their quarterly instalments of
Puffin Post, which is now back for a new generation.

Many years from now, we hope you'll look back and
remember Puffin with a smile. **No matter what your age
or what you're into, there's a Puffin for everyone.**
The possibilities are endless, but one thing is for sure:
whether it's a picture book or a paperback, a sticker book
or a hardback, **if it's got that little Puffin
on it – it's bound to be good.**